I0627906

LIES, SEX

&

BETRAYAL

Denecia Green

Lies, Sex & Betrayal

Published by Denecia Green

Copyright © 2014 by Denecia Green

ISBN 978-1-949343-16-8

Acknowledgment

My dream of writing an adult novel has finally been realized, and I am deeply grateful to God for the gifts he has allowed this journey to bring into my life. He has blessed me in spite of myself and I am humbled by his grace.

To my family, thanks for your undying love, support and encouragement to follow my dreams; your kind words and gentle nudges catapulted me to new heights.

Many thanks to Christopher Serju and Ms. Stacey A Palmer, my editor, for your listening ear and literary suggestions that thickened the plot and made my words come to life. To Jonathan Cooke, you are a talented Web designer and Geovanni Hinds, a very skilled photographer. Thank you both for creating such an aesthetically pleasing cover.

To my readers, thank you so much for the never-ending support you have shown me. You could have done many things with your hard-earned dollars; I am appreciative that you used them to purchase this book and I hope that you enjoy it.

Also by Denecia Green

Life: Through A Teen's Eyes

A compilation of short stories capturing the life of typical modern teenagers from various socioeconomic backgrounds. The range of stories cover light hearted experiences such as the first kiss, the power of generosity as well as more heavy-set experiences, including dealing with death, abuse and drug addiction. The stories are intended to inspire and guide readers on how to deal with a few challenges of life.

Love, Lies & Temptation (Sequel to Lies, Sex & Betrayal)

Briana and Kim are best friends in their early twenties struggling to navigate their daily lives. Amidst their desire for carnal pleasures and their drive to achieve professional success lie many temptations designed to veer them off track. The two friends, who have both made major mistakes in their personal lives, find themselves wanting more than what they have.

With many heartbreaks under her belt and a relatively successful career, Briana happens upon love in an unexpected place and from the most unlikely man. Finally, she is settled and happy, and everything could not go any better for her. Kim on the other hand, gives up true love and long-term peace of mind for the financial riches she has always yearned. The catch is that she will have to sell her soul to the devil to maintain it. In the end, the only thing the two friends have left in common is their love and devotion to each other, but they end up on opposite ends of the happiness spectrum.

FROM THE BEGINNING

By: Bad Bitch

"What the fuck?" Budu shouted as he jumped out of bed, waking me. I sat up and watched as he searched frantically through the drawers and under the mattress. BOOM!! CRASH! BANG!! My heart jumped at the sound of glass crashing and metal smashing. "Babe, what's happening?"

There was no answer as he continued searching.

"Ahh fuck! Kim I told you to stop moving my shit." My heart pounded against the merino threatening to jump loose of my chest. Budu was a drug dealer and may have committed a few crimes in his lifetime, but I was ok with this. He was paying the bills, buying the groceries, in addition to giving me $20,000 every week so I was happy. I liked nice things, and Budu made sure I got whatever I wanted whenever I wanted it. He had a crew of young boys on the streets who did most of the work, so the chances of him getting caught were slim, but apparently some heavy shit was gonna go down today. Damn, someone must have snitched. It was either those jealous motherfuckers from our rival community or the police bastards who had a vendetta against my man. Suddenly, I was aware of a loud banging on the door; my heart skipped a beat, as I heard the thunder of feet heading in our direction.

Next minute I was staring up the wrong end of an MP5, as the realization hit home that we were fucked!

"On the floor, get the fuck on the floor," I heard, watching as Budu raised his hands, folding them behind his head and assumed the position. His body suddenly slammed into the floor as two of the policemen kicked and kneed him in the back. The scream which started deep in my bowels was aborted long before reaching my lips as I found myself being cuffed, and my face pressed against the damn wall.

"Tear this fucking place up until we find some shit," one of the bastards bellowed. I turned my head just in time to see his massive boot crash into my lover's side, again and again. Closing my eyes hard in an effort to block the scene from my mind, I was suddenly aware of the noise of them ripping our apartment apart, kicking down furniture, tossing my clothes, accessories, laptop, picture frame and just about every damn thing on the floor. We had worked so hard to build our mini mansion, and these motherfuckers were taking a perverse pleasure in destroying the fruits of our labour. I had been cuffed for so long that I started to feel the circulation in my hands going and a deep tiredness began to take over my body. I was quickly yanked back to reality, biting my lips as despair mingled with anger at the next thing I heard.

"Look at these sexy panties," the pervert grunted, moving his face closer and taking three long, exaggerated sniffs before proudly declaring, "Ahh, the smell of pretty pussy." My humiliation increased when he walked over to Budu and I could visualize the leering as that bastard continued with his dirty talk. "I think I will fuck your woman while you rot in prison. Better yet, why don't I fuck her right here and now? I know she would like that with you watching."

Before I had enough time to process what the asshole was saying, I felt his hand on my shoulder pulling me forward; his other grabbed my crotch painfully hard and my reflexes kicked in, so I spat in my assailant's face. My victory was short lived as I crashed to the floor, realizing only then that he too had acted on instincts. I heard the sound before I felt the pain; his hands crashing against my jawbone echoed in my head, and I felt like the floor had come up and meet me.

Tasting blood, I still found the strength to taunt him, my breath coming in gasps as I struggled to speak with my face kissing the cold tiles, as a mega headache kicked in.

"You fucking police are worse than the criminals," I managed to spit out.

"Keep talking bitch and I really will give you something to regret," he shot back, a combat boot stamping my ample ass, while the nozzle of a rifle caressed my neck. This was definitely not the time to play hero, I decided.

Budu was definitely fucked. They had found the two shotguns and AK47 rifle left over from a sales meeting the night before. I had told him to hurry and sell that shit, now it was too late. As they hauled him off the floor roughly and shoved him toward the waiting police vehicle, tears welled in my eyes.

STORMY IN THE HOUSE OF THE LORD

By: Temptress

He did not dress like a deacon nor did he go around preaching to people about how they should live. In fact, he was like no other clergy man I had ever known., Brother Mario's singing and expertise on the drums were like a magic spell, mesmerizing, as he did, the young people in our church with his talents. Each Sunday, I looked forward to him conducting praise and worship and whenever he sang, that man sent chills down my spine. Recently saved, baptized and filled with the Holy Ghost, it wasn't just his heartrending rendition of Cece Winan's 'Mercy Said No' that resulted in the older women weeping and wailing and causing the young girls to lust after him. Truth be told, every girl wanted a guy who could sing.

From the first day, all the young girls in the church competed for Mario's attention and after he was given the 14-19 class to teach at Sunday school they suddenly became more attentive. The transformation among the sisters continued but not in the way I think the church elders anticipated; skirts and dresses started getting shorter and shorter. Some of my friends even gave up regular stockings for fish net stockings and began dressing in heels they could hardly manage to walk in. Sunday services were really heating up, and I began to be entertained by the ridiculous antics of all these righteous women and girls fighting for Mario's attention.

Alicia got the goodly pastor to agree to spend time with her after church one Sunday, on the pretext that she needed further help in understanding certain sections of the Book of Revelations. This was not lost on Jodi, who was in a foul mood, when it became apparent that her friend had won some quality time with the object of our mutual affection.

That evening, instead of heading home as usual, I found excuses to hang around, determined that whatever happened, I would be there to witness. Bibles in hand, Alicia and Mario sat very close to each other as they read chapters, discussed the issues for what seem like hours and before you knew it, the church yard was empty, all the goodly Christians having left. With that realization, the couple became more relaxed. Before long, I was enjoying a peep show unlike anything I had seen before.

When Mario let his hands brush her thighs, resting there a little longer than necessary, Alicia got fidgety and giggly but did nothing to stop him. As if emboldened by this show of tacit approval, he made the next big move. Slowly getting up, he headed to the back of the church, beckoning for his young charge to follow. Determined not to be left out of the action, I carefully followed, staying well out of sight but close enough to catch everything.

Now safely out of the view of prying eyes, Mario leaned against a wall, stretched out a hand and gently pulled Alicia close. It was evident that she was nervous, which made him unsure of just how to proceed. That did not stop him though; he tenderly brushed her hair with one hand and drew her forward with the other, kissing first her forehead, then eyes and lips. They both grew in confidence, and when Mario passionately crushed her lips with his, Alicia was ready, giving as good as she got, opening wide to receive his tongue. Then her knees seemed to buckle and Brother Mario used the opportunity to catch and hold her, his hands slipping up her skirt and driving my friend to what appeared to be new heights of pleasure.

Alicia was now gasping for air but soon regained control as she slowly stepped back holding Brother Mario at arm's length, a big smile on her face. "Your kisses were just like I had imagined, Mario" she managed to say. "I'm going to head home now. Thanks for helping me understand today's lesson," Alicia continued innocently. Mario grabbed her by the arms as she walked away. "I have something additional for you, let me just get it from the office."

"Brother Mario," a voice shouted. "You are still here? I was about to lock up."

"I'll be here for a little while. I want to get the notes right for the solo I will be performing later. Can you come back in about one hour?"

"Sure, I will be next door, so just signal me when you are ready," the caretaker hollered back.

"Ok no prob."

I ran up the stairs and hid in the pastor's study determined not to miss Mario's gift presentation to Alicia. My heart pounded so fast and hard that I found it difficult to breathe. I stared at the cross on the wall where Jesus hung. "Briana what are you doing…?" My conscience began to pick an argument with me." Getting a little nervous, I decided to leave them alone and head home to catch up on studies and well overdue assignments. I looked around the study one last time but as I turned to open the door, I saw Mario and Alicia strutting down the hallway towards me. I nervously scrambled into the closet, and I buried myself in the corner and peeked through the opening in the closet just in time to see Mario close the room door and drop the keys into his pocket.

"What are you doing Mario?" asked Alicia, sounding slightly frightened. I swallowed a big ball of saliva and tried to calm down. I was so nervous. Mario then placed his hands over her mouth and nose so she couldn't breathe. What happened next caught us both completely off guard. "If you scream I will kill you." It took some time for me to realize that those cold, menacing words were coming from the man we had all come to adore. I felt a trickle of pee start down my leg as he roughly pulled off Alicia's stockings and panty. Confusion turned to panic and I prayed he would not find me. Next thing I knew Alicia was on the floor and Mario was straddling her, pulling her legs apart as he struggled to penetrate her. "Mario….no…please stop," she screamed as he drove forward, grunting in pleasure with each movement, as she tried in vain to push him away.

"Now that was some good pussy." At the sound of his voice I realized I had actually closed my eyes sometime during the ordeal and was jolted back to reality just in time to see Mario grab the stockings and use them to wipe his penis. Despite the heat, Alicia lay shivering on the floor, looking numb as her virginity bled down her thighs and on to the floor of the Pastor's study. But Mario wasn't finished humiliating her. "First time feeling a big cock in that tight, sweet pussy of yours, huh? Don't worry though you are going to be one of those bitches who love to fuck." There was no response from Alicia. It didn't even seem like she was breathing. She lay very still on the floor. "Alicia?" he kicked her legs and even though there was still no response that didn't seem to bother her rapist. "I always noticed you and Jodi competing to get my attention, sitting with your legs slightly opened, just enough for me to see your pussies, wearing extra make up and miniskirts, dressing like little sluts, batting your eyelashes, flirting and shit and now that you have my attention you are not talking." He curled his lips in disgust.

"Let me tell you something Alicia, pussy was created for fucking and having babies. So don't be thinking I did you wrong. I merely prepared you. And don't be thinking of telling anyone I raped you. Once you're fucking back it's not considered rape so get that in your little head. You need to get off the damn floor and stop feeling sorry for yourself. Clean up this mess and go home." He stepped over her and unlocked the doors, breaking out into "Nobody greater, nobody greater, Lord nobody greater than you," Alicia's innocence still ripe on his dick. After he left, Alicia picked up her red cotton panties and stepped into them. Taking up the soiled stockings she used them to wipe the blood from her legs and then used them to clean the floor.

Afterwards, she gingerly slipped into her dress and put on her shoes before feebly walking out of the office.

I'm surprised I didn't suffer a heart attack. I had stopped breathing for what seemed like 30 minutes. I still could not believe that I had just witnessed the transformation of a man believed to be baptized and filled with the Holy Ghost, into the worst kind of devil anyone could imagine. The debonair gentleman I had watched on Sundays, revealed to be a callous rapist who, after viciously assaulting an innocent 16-year old girl, went on to abuse her mentally and hum a gospel song without skipping a beat. Where was his conscience? How could he do such a thing? Why didn't God stop him? Then it dawned on me that I had been there. Why didn't I stop him? Why didn't I help? What should I do now? Do I pretend that nothing happened, or tell someone? Should I let Alicia know that I was aware of what had happened? Lord what should I do? The questions I asked myself were too many and I felt like my mind was about to explode. After checking to make sure they both had gone, I slowly left the pastor's study and ran out of the church yard as fast as I could. I thought church was different. I didn't expect a Christian to be doing those things. As I journeyed home, I reflected on the various men in the church in high positions. Were they sleeping with members of the congregation too? Were they raping young girls or were they dating men? My head started hurting with the many unanswered questions circulating. This incident scarred me for good. Christianity was not what I had perceived it to be.

ROCK BOTTOM

By: Bad Bitch

After hours of questioning, I was released because I had no criminal record but Budu was fucked. Both of us, it seemed, because with him in jail there was no way I could now afford to maintain the lifestyle to which I was addicted. I rushed home to see if I could retrieve anything.

Budu had a little safe in the bedroom which contained our life savings. The plan was that I could live off that for some time, or until he was released... ... who knows when he would be. So maybe I would just live of the savings until the money ran out. It was something we had discussed after a previous run-in with the law, and he had promised then to make provisions for my survival if the law ever caught up with him. I swallowed hard as I entered the bedroom and slid open the doors to the closet. My chest started heaving, and my entire body became numb. I couldn't breathe. I could see where the curtain had been peeled back and the big hole in the floor that usually contained the safe was empty. The fucking police had taken the money, my Rolex and everything of value. I am sure they had pocketed all that shit.

Noooooo!!!!! I screamed, holding my head. I only had about $5,000 in my purse which couldn't do shit to me. I had gotten so used to spending that on one pair of shoes. I sat in the same position for what seemed like a lifetime. My eyes were swollen, my throat was sore and my head thumped, as I tried to come to terms with what happened.

I had to get a job. I would settle for any job as long as it didn't get me into trouble with the law. Secondly, I was done dating men like Budu. This was a wake up call. I knew I was going to miss the fancy life but promised myself I would never do drugs or date criminals anymore. I looked around at what was left of the life I had taken for granted. I grabbed a few bags and stuffed whatever I could inside. This was probably as close as I would ever get, for a while, to wearing designer clothing.

My next thought was to find a place to stay and I realized the best option was to move back in with my parents. Hopefully they would not ask too many questions. I had hit rock bottom. It was time to start a new life and get things right this time around.

SAINT.......TO SINNER

By: Temptress

I wish I had not stayed back after church that day. I was scarred for life. I couldn't eat because thoughts of blood trickling down Alicia's legs and the way he manhandled her constantly harassed my mind. The moment I closed my eyes all the events of that evening replayed over and over. I was scared, disgusted, confused and paranoid. I didn't know who to trust. I needed to talk to someone but didn't think anyone would believe that a well-respected believer would do such a thing. Instead, I let my thoughts concerning the gruesome events of that fateful Sunday bottle up and consume my beliefs, happiness and anything in relation to church. That was the last day for me at that so-called house of God. From that moment, NO ONE...could get me to go NEAR, much less inside a church. There were constant phone calls from members of the church, deacons and others, all concerned about the fact that I had suddenly stopped coming to church and trying to get me back on track. But nothing worked, because there was no way I was going anywhere near that place again.

Whenever I was on the road and glimpsed a member of the church, I made sure to avoid eye contact or would just simply change my route. I was not about to have a conversation with any one of them, especially in public. One thing I learned was that church people really did not know when to stop. The minute they start talking about the Bible it takes a miracle to shut them up. Funny enough Brother Mario also approached me one day at the Mall and had the audacity to lecture me about "walking the straight and narrow." I wanted to strangle him. He just proved to me how much of a hypocrite people could be. I had to abruptly stop him in his lecture and walk off. The hypocrisy was too much. How dare he lecture me about Christianity when he had raped an innocent girl on the church grounds? I know we all have our flaws or weaknesses and make mistakes but there was no way I was going to just forgive and forget easily. Although it hadn't happen to me, the fact that I witnessed it definitely had an impact on my mind set. I, who once enjoyed singing on the choir, ministering in dance to Christ, and conducting praise and worship, now explored gyrating on men, partying, alcohol and all the other possible desires of the flesh.

This became even easier way of life for me, when I started nursing school. Drinking, partying and promiscuity were rampant on campus. Although I no longer attended church, I was still slightly reserved about engaging these activities. Amidst all this I still pledged to save my virginity for my husband. That was one resolution I was sticking to. I guess there was some truth to the old saying, train up a child in the way he should go and when he gets old he will not depart from it.

I also had a boyfriend who happened to be the son of a pastor. Even though we never had sex, we did several things I am sure God would not have been proud of. The hypocrisy of being a sinner Monday to Saturdays then a Holy Ghost-filled believer on Sunday was exactly how my boyfriend operated; he perpetuated the same lifestyle I despised Brother Mario for living. Now, here I was several months later doing the same thing with a pastor's son.

The life of the party, the real drama queen was the life I chose to live and had no regrets. I made a very easy transformation from saint to sinner.

TRYING TO FIGURE SHIT OUT

By: Bad Bitch

"Alright Kim, you got this," I whispered, running my hands down my Antonio Melano pencil skirt to smooth out the wrinkles. Then I turned towards the half broken bathroom mirror to check out my ass and beautiful face. These were my best assets and I planned to use them in every way to get ahead in life. I couldn't make it out of my misery via academia. Didn't have the patience or skill, so I was going to work with what I have; my body. I puckered my lips and headed out on my quest to find a job.

I went from cosmetic stores, to clothing, shoes, make up stores, even pharmacies, without success. This shit was hard. It seemed next to impossible to get a job even though I was well dressed in my designer clothing.

After hours of walking the streets, my life began to flash before my eyes – memories of the police banging on the doors, hauling me against the wall in cuffs and throwing my prized possessions across the house. My chest tightened as I reminisced. It's been an entire week and I hadn't received a single phone call from Budu. I wondered what was happening with him but was afraid to visit. I didn't want to be the girlfriend waiting on her man to get out of prison. I was running as far away as possible from that lifestyle.

I needed a place to quickly recompose myself and headed to a fast food joint to get something to eat. It was as if for the first time I really noticed the people around me; people working and selling things as simple as baby wipes just to earn an income. I guess I was so caught up in my fast-paced life, being handed everything so easily and as often as I needed, I didn't really know what it felt like to not have things my way. It had been like this for as long as I could remember. Even my parents had threatened to put me out the house as a teenager because I was always disrespectful, disobedient and caustic towards them.

I also had my fair share of dick, having been sexually active from age 14. I was fucking wealthy business men, high level criminals, married men, just about all types of men that walked this earth. I loved getting money and material things, and the men knew this, so the more they gave, the wider my legs opened. I called myself a bad bitch.

Unfortunately, I got pregnant but got rid of that fucking baggage so fast it wasn't even funny. I wasn't about to let a baby slow me down. I had a lot of shit going on and a baby did not fit into that equation.

I took a bite into the hamburger and was drawn back to reality. Now here I was from being a rich bitch, to a broke motherfucker trying to figure shit out.

With all that was happening, it would be more difficult to survive on my own, so I called my parents and asked permission to move back in.

Thankfully, they welcomed me whole- heartedly back into their home, being the good Christian people they are. They never even questioned it. I was like the prodigal's daughter. I finished my lunch then headed back home to pack to move in with my parents. Tomorrow I would do it all over again. I wasn't giving up easily.

COLLEGE CHRONICLES

By: Temptress

After three months of summer holidays, it was time to prepare for yet another stressful semester. Fortunately I managed to score As and Bs in all my courses and had successfully complete my second year of nursing school. I quickly looked through the final year syllabus which seemed to be more practical than theoretical. This was a relief as I preferred hands-on experience. I was finally about to start feeling like a nurse and got really excited about final year.

My attention shifted to a group of ladies who entered the premises dressed in clothing that didn't seem to comfortably host their body parts. One looked like her breast would pop out if she sneezed. The whole auditorium became silent the minute they walked by. At least they provided a brief moment of entertainment, because we were becoming restless from waiting so long for the start of the meeting to which third year students had been invited.

As I patiently waited, I had nothing better to do than criticize the outfits of passersby as well as every vehicle that pulled into the parking lot, trying to figure out which was the chairman. Finally, a red Range Rover Evoque pulled into the parking lot. I was eager to see whether the driver looked as attractive as the vehicle. My friend Mia nudged me as well after seeing the

Rover because she had this petty theory that ugly men drove nice cars. With our gazed fixed on the vehicle, a man who looked like no taller than 5-foot exited it.

"What the heck is a short man like him doing with such a big vehicle?" Mia blurted out. I slapped her and beckoned for her to behave as the man was heading in our direction. I scrutinized him from head to toe. He was short but a ten in my eyes. I loved a man who knew how to put an outfit together and wear it well. He was wearing a navy jacket with brass buttons, slim sleeves that revealed about an inch of shirt cuff, slim cut woollen pants with a pair of loafers that anchored his outfit with easy sophistication. I loved his attire, and I made it obvious. I smiled and flirtatiously looked away as soon as our eyes met.

I waited for a few minutes before returning my stare, hoping he would not be looking at me but he was. "Briana, stop staring" Mia said, as she elbowed me. The gentleman was now heading in our direction.

"See what you caused," she said as he approached us. Though very close friends, Mia and I were opposites. She was shy and more the type to follow the conventional strategy of waiting for a man to compliment a woman and make the first move. I, on the other hand, wasn't afraid of making the first move. One thing I had learnt about men, especially men of authority, was to flatter their ego.

I was not only more outspoken than Mia but also a flirt. I didn't hesitate to say how sexy he looked in his carefully tailored outfit. A quirk of mine was men who spoke very well and had a strong command of the

English Language. His diction was flawless coupled with the fact that he had nicely aligned pearly white teeth. Nice Lips and teeth were two additional quirks of mine as it relates to men.

"You are quite outspoken for a girl your age," he said.

"That's a good quality to have though," he further stated. We conversed until the chairman arrived for the meeting. I was furious that he showed up during a crucial point in our conversation. I was enjoying every second of my new friend's time. We exchanged numbers, and then he left me to my meeting.

I thought about my new acquaintance the whole time. I couldn't wait to talk with him again and called as soon as I got home. We spoke for hours. I was so engrossed in the conversation I didn't even want to answer my boyfriend's telephone calls but eventually did anyway for the sake of avoiding an extensive interrogation from him. It was routine for him to be with me or for us to engage in long telephone conversations when I was not at school unless I had chores or had to study. He knew my schedule.

Originally, my boyfriend and I had planned to catch a movie that night but at the last minute he cancelled. I was really disappointed because this was its final week. I told Alex about it hoping he would volunteer to see it with me, and my plan actually worked.

DATE NIGHT

By: Temptress

I was more nervous than a virgin in a whorehouse, because I had never been out with anyone other than my boyfriend over the last three years. I was also nervous about meeting with someone I had only known for six hours. As a result, I decided to meet him at the theatre instead of him picking me up at home. I had a knot in my stomach the whole time on the way to the theatre. What would people think? He was noticeably older than I was, and I worried about coming across as stupid or immature in his presence. With several quick deep breaths, I silenced my thoughts before entering the theatre.

He got there before I did and bought popcorn, nachos and jumbo sodas. We basically had enough food to last through out the movie. I liked the fact that he didn't try to make any move towards me. We LITERALLY watched the movie. I enjoyed his company and the movie. He offered to take me home. I barely knew him but already felt comfortable in his presence.

As we journeyed home, I couldn't help but wonder what would happen if David called? I was a terrible liar, so it wouldn't take much for him to realize that something was different. David was the only lover I had ever had. While I didn't think he was an exceptional lover, I didn't have anyone to compare him to. I probably wasn't exceptional myself. I was a very sheltered child who rarely went out and was not exposed to many things until I met David. He was my first in most things. He taught me how to kiss and introduced me to various restaurants, concerts and parties. I was very timid when it came to sex. The three years we had been together we never had sex and he never pressured me. That was one of the many things I loved about him. I had gathered enough courage to watch some pornography with him on a few occasions. Although it made me uncomfortable at times, I figured it was the least I could do so I wouldn't make a fool of myself when the time came. The private conversation in my head was interrupted by Alex suggesting that we stop at his house for a few minutes. My heart skipped a beat as a gazillion thoughts rushed through my head. I guess he sensed this and tried to reassure me. I flashed a half smile then managed to mumble the word "ok" but a long awkward moment of silence followed.

I was in awe and fought hard to hold back my amazement. I had never before seen a house of this size. This man seemed to be very wealthy. I scrutinized the two ornate bronze metal gates, set in a six-foot high sandstone wall. I watched closely as Alex pressed a button on the Rover's door handle and the electric window hummed quietly down into the doorframe. He punched a number into the keypad and the gates swung open in welcome. As we pulled up into the driveway, I was greeted by a mini waterfall cascading into a pond filled with fish. I was already captivated by the outward appearance of his house and couldn't wait to view the inside.

As we entered through the front door, I saw an imposing U-shaped white sofa that could seat 10 adults comfortably. It faced a state-of-the-art stainless steel or maybe platinum for all I know, modern fireplace, which was lit. On the right was the kitchen area with dark wood marble work tops and a large breakfast bar which seated eight. Across from the kitchen area was a dining table surrounded by 16 chairs and tucked in the corner were two large statues. I didn't quite fathom the setting but assumed it must have been something with a profound historical background. There was art of all shapes and sizes on the walls. This living room looked more like an art gallery than a place to live. There was also the entertainment centre that hosted what seemed like a 50-inch LED smart television with surround sound, complemented by a sofa bed. These were things I only dreamed of purchasing, things Alex clearly had at his disposal.

I then journeyed upstairs to the master bedroom which was quite interesting. My attention was fixed on the several nude paintings that lined the head of the bed. He had a king size bed, lined with curtains that had an opening at the front. However, what I found intriguing was the ability to manipulate the intensity of the light with just a turn of a knob. I then strolled into the bathroom that was bigger than my bedroom at home, with grey, white and blue marble in an attractive pattern. It was stocked with all the luxuries you would expect from the suite of a 5-star hotel; mini bottles of body lotion, shampoo, conditioner, shower gel as well as soap, grooming kits, shower caps in little pastel boxes that look so gorgeous it would be a shame to open them. I look longingly at the sparkling clean oval Jacuzzi with built in speakers on the outside. There was also a shower with glass doors. I opened them only to be greeted by numerous buttons. I must have had a puzzled look on my face because it wasn't long before Alex maneuvred the different buttons. There were tiny holes all around that could produce water from whatever direction you liked. One button was responsible for controlling the direction of the water. Other switches controlled the temperature, the amount of water or whether you wanted music. I think my eyes must have lit up like a child receiving a new toy because I was truly fascinated. When I finally managed to suppress my amazement, he had a smirk on his face which made me feel a little embarrassed. I then peered over the balcony where I saw a pool, lawn chairs, a hammock and what seemed like a gym and a pool house. I loved his house.

I became a bit more relaxed after light conversation while touring his mansion. We talked for about another hour; after which, he took me home.

DEALING WITH MY DEMONS

By: Bad Bitch

Day 2 of job hunting, and I was drained. I left resumes at just about any and every business enterprise; most of which told me that there were no vacancies but I left the resumes anyway. My options were limited. I strolled into a pharmacy and traversed the aisles, as I took advantage of air conditioning. A gentleman who appeared to be restocking the shelves drew my attention; he was sharp. His hair was cut perfectly and the jewellery looked expensive. His chin was square with a dimple smack dab in the middle, perfect cheeks and his lips were huge. I couldn't stop staring at the huge scar that ran from his chiselled jawbone down the side of his neck. I found him sexually appealing. I glimpsed his name tag and with the words manager scribbled beneath his name. Maybe this was my chance to make it happen, so I approached him.

I picked up something from the shelf and deliberately threw it on the floor in his direction. Bending to pick up the item, I deliberately parted my legs, exposing my bare pussy. I paused for a few seconds before getting up, watching his gaze fixed between my legs. I watched him from the corner of my eye as I gently replaced the item on the shelf, and then took a step backwards, pretending to scrutinize it.

"Is there anything I can help you with?" he asked.

"No, thank you."

"I am Mr Williams. You can call me Jemar," he said extending his arm for a handshake.

"I am Kim. Nice to meet you Jemar," I said, flashing a half smile.

"Is there anything in particular you are trying to find? I just may be able to assist you."

"Actually there is one thing. I have been trying to get a job but nothing has materialized as yet. Would it be possible for you to consider me for any vacancies here in the future?"

"We are actually seeking someone to relieve our cashier who is heavily pregnant. Would you be interested in that type of job?"

"I will settle for anything right now."

He laughed. "Well follow me to the office so we can discuss the matter further."

I smiled and breathed a sigh of relief. This was my lucky day.

I looked around the office and couldn't help but notice the pictures on the wall in which he was standing with another man, very likely father and son. The resemblance was a dead giveaway. It seemed he had a bit of affluence to his name, so I needed to get my shit together in a hurry. Timed right, a few minutes of sweaty fucking could lead to a lifetime of money, jewellery and vacations. The need to have material things was my demon. I said I was done with that kind of life but needed badly to start really living again.

"Do you have any experience as a cashier Kim?" I was drawn back to the present by Jemar's voice.

"Well no, but I learn quickly and I am more than willing to work free for a few days just to learn what is required of me, provided that this is ok with you? I will work with whatever you want," I continued, shooting him a flirtatious glance.

"It would be very inappropriate of me to really tell you what I want, so let's…" he chuckled. I laughed. "We just may want the same things but you will never know until you ask, I said, unfolding my legs and biting my lips. I watched his eyes stray between my legs once more, as he eased back in the chair and loosened his tie. "You are making this interview very difficult for me Kim." Leaning across the table I kissed him full on the lips. Shocked, he pulled away but I wasn't giving up and continued with my advances. Before long we were atop the table and ripping off each other's clothes. Unbuckling his pants he sank his dick hungrily into my pussy and we proceeded to fuck with vengeance. I returned his pumps for as long as I could before cuming. Panting, and out of breath, I didn't know what I had just done, randomly fucking this guy just so I could get a lousy nine to five job.

"Alright Kim, you start on Monday. We start at 8:30," he finally managed to mutter.

That was some good shit, I must admit. I scribbled my number on the notepad, took up my belongings and tried earnestly to compose myself. My legs were a bit wobbly as I looked back at Jemar one last time before unlocking the door and winked as I left.

I had gotten the job, and that was all that mattered.

THE REUNION

By: Bad Bitch

When I got home mom told me a young man by the name of Bugz had left a number for me to call. I was taken aback as I tried to figure out how he had gotten my number or knew where I was staying. My mind went wild as I tried to figure out why Bugz had contacted me. He was one of Budu's closest friends, and I had not heard from any of them since the ordeal. I returned the call and held my breath.

"Hey Kim, long time don't see?"

"What do you want?" I quickly blurtted out of fear. "Not even a 'hi, how are you?' What did I ever do to you Kim?"

"Sorry, I am just a little nervous."

"Ok. I understand. Well I wanted to meet with you tonight. I am having a little get together at my girlfriend's house and would like to catch up on old times."

"Anything old, I would like to stay that way," I said sternly.

"Ouch...that was harsh. Well the invite is still open if you change your mind. The address is 72 Sunshine

Place. I really hope to see you. Enjoy the rest of your day Kim." He hung up without not even giving me time to respond.

Should I really go tonight....was he up to something...maybe he knows something about Budu? Curiosity was wearing me out. Why had Bugz contacted me all of a sudden? Eventually I decided I would go but not spend more than one hour.

I searched for a provocative dress. I wanted Bugz and his girlfriend to realize that I was doing well on my own without Budu. After all, they were accustomed to me looking a certain way, so I had to uphold my reputation regardless of how things were.

In the meantime I had a heart to heart talk with both parents and enjoyed every moment of it. It had been a mighty long time since we had talked like this. I was just surprised they didn't despise me after the hell I put them through. They were happy I was working. My mother asked who Bugz was and questioned his name? I couldn't refrain from laughing. No matter how grown you are, a good mother will forever be concerned. I told her that he was an old friend from high school who somehow found out I was back at home. I didn't want to start lying to my mother all over again, but then I didn't think she needed to know my dirty secrets just yet. I did not think it would surprise her but preferred to keep her believing I had changed somewhat into the woman she had always wanted me to become. After our talk, I had dinner, got dressed and headed to Bugz's place.

****

It was a nice little apartment which suggested they were still living the life. Bugz's girlfriend, Anastasia, looked like a million dollars as usual. I greeted her with a smack on the cheeks. "It's so good to see you again Kim, I am glad you could make it." She handed me a glass of wine and proceeded to greet her other guests. Bugz then rushed up and lifted me off the ground. I must say I was happy to see everyone again.

"You look fine as usual" Bugz said. "Thank you," I said smiling.

"Come with me." I placed my hands in his and followed him to another room.

"Ahhh" I uttered as I sat in the big comfy sofas that adjusted to my body. Bugz sized me up then laughed.

"Make yourself at home. So how are you?"

"I am good." I said.

"Kim, I mean HOW ARE YOU?" he reiterated.

"I miss Budu but there is nothing I can do about that so I am letting him and that life go and moving forward. I haven't heard from him since the bust."

"Well I haven't spoken to him in a while. You know we don't want to raise any more suspicions. Plus, we are still trying to figure out who the informant was; I suppose he is doing all he can behind bars. After all, he was sentenced to 10 years so…"

My eyes welled up with tears. I really loved Budu, so it's just unfortunate that things had to unfold this way. "You know I got you though Kim, whatever you need just say it. Do you need money, when last have you been shopping? I know how much you loved your designer shit." We both laughed. "I appreciate the offer but I am ok. I have a job and…. "You have a what?" he said stopping me mid sentence. "Get the fuck outta here. YOU KIM who says she wants nothing but to be kept, has a job? Oh man, how I wish Budu was here to see this."

"If Budu was here I wouldn't have to do this," I said, slightly irritated. There was a brief pause. My eyes drifted across to the counter once again "I am sorry. As I said, if there is anything you need, I am here….ANYTHING," he repeated, "including whatever you keep looking at on the counter." I was slightly embarrassed by the fact that he noticed. I had not had cocaine in so long, I tried to imagine the smell and taste of it. No Kim, no…I told myself. Remember you are burying your demons, you are starting fresh.

Anastasia came bursting through the door. "Is everything ok in here? You both should come party with us outside." I watched intently as she headed to the counter, neatly prepared a line from the stash and sniffed that baby so quickly. I felt myself float for a couple seconds as I imagined the euphoria she must be experiencing. I glanced at Bugz only to see him watching me with a smile plastered on his face. I took up my glass of wine and headed back with Anastasia. The minute I got to where the music and excitement was, I found a seat and watched the girls. They were very entertaining. Some clearly were already drunk.

Anastasia stood on the table in the centre of the room, flung her hands in the air and moved her body sensually. It wasn't long before Bugz joined her, rubbing his crotch against her ass as they gyrated. Anastasia then grabbed my hand, inviting me to dance with her. I was hesitant but after a while joined her. "I know what will loosen you up," Anastasia whispered in my ear. She grabbed my hands and that of a very attractive Indian girl, hauled us both into the room. Without saying a word she shoved me onto the sofa, pulled my dress down, leaving my breasts fully exposed, took a handful of cocaine and placed it on my chest then buried her face between my breasts and snorted that powder like her nose was a vacuum cleaner. Then she licked me from nipple to nipple, flicking her tongue roughly over my erect breasts. By this time the other girl had lifted Anastasia's skirt and was eating her pussy from behind. That drove me wild. I fingered my clitoris as I watched and listened to Anastasia moaning as the girl ate her. I was so horny. Anastasia then repeated the procedure with the cocaine but this time on my clit. She sucked on my clit like a baby with pacifier. I could feel my chest heaving with excitement. Anastasia used her hands to part the lips. She then sank her piercing tongue into my hot, wet pussy, flicking in and out with a dizzying rhythm. Throwing my head back, I closed my eyes as she went to work. I felt cum welling up in my loins and realizing I was about to explode, I grabbed her head forcefully and pushed her farther into my pussy. Stopping suddenly, she jumped up and as I cried out in anguish and looked up with questioning eyes, I saw Bugz dick in hand as he slipped on a condom. I didn't know what was happening, had not bargained for any of it but was enjoying myself so much, I wasn't stopping for anything. I screamed with pleasure as his dick revved up the pleasure Anastasia had started, pumping up and down. Just then Anastasia covered my mouth with her pussy and I didn't disappoint her, giving as good as I got, nibbling on her cunt, as her boyfriend rammed me. Just before he came, Bugz pull off the condom shooting his load all over my face and Anastasia's pussy. The other girl then started licking his cum off my chin. I had never felt so good in my life. It was also my first encounter with women but I liked it. All my years of fucking men for money, positions and drugs, I had never had this kind of experience or orgasm, not even with Budu. It felt like I was in some kind of heaven, well maybe not the one saints go to, but this certainly wasn't hell. I couldn't move from the sofa. I watched as Anastasia cleaned up and left the room with the other girl. Bugz and I were spent. We chatted until all the other guests left, and he later took me home. This was certainly a reunion to remember.

THE FIRST TIME

By: Temptress

Things had changed between David and I, and the slightest thing triggered a fuss. When I didn't argue back, that too became an issue. He interpreted this to mean I did not care enough about our relationship to defend it and eventually stopped pushing. There came a point where we did not speak for about a week, but it didn't affect me as much because I was buried in meeting deadlines for numerous group projects and course work that was long overdue. I sensed the distance but really could not channel my energy in that direction at the moment. Thankfully, David came to his senses and tried to be more understanding with all I had going on at school that week. He apologized for fussing with me unnecessarily and suggested making it up to me that weekend.

David's parents were going out of town so we agreed to spend the time at their house. He picked out several movies and even though I had seen most of them already, I didn't mind watching again. He prepared a meal of boiled dumplings and canned mackerel for our lunch. It wasn't a fancy meal, but he knew how much I loved mackerel so it was a good gesture and I was more than satisfied.

"Babe, you never told me how the movie was the other day? Who did you go with?" he asked from the kitchen.

"It was good. I went with Mia," I responded quickly, focussing on clearing the table.

"I am really sorry I couldn't make it," he said, placing his arms around my waist kissing me gently on the forehead. "That's ok. You are here now and we have all weekend together. Let's just make the most of it," I said.

I cleaned up after lunch and watched him sprawled out on the sofa, glued to the television. I really wasn't comfortable around him of late and had been having misgivings, suspicions about him messing with another woman but just couldn't quite put my fingers on it. But then the fact that he was being so nice and nothing had really changed between us made me shrug off these insecurities.

I quickly finished up in the kitchen and joined him on the sofa. "You know I care about you right?" He ran his fingers through my hair, then raised my chin with his index finger and proceeded to lay a long, wet kiss on my lips. "Let me make love to you tonight." He ran his hands slowly and gently along my thighs. I always have this tingly feeling inside whenever he touched my thighs. I really did not know what to say. "Is that what you really want?" I lovingly gazed up into his eyes.

"Nothing would make me happier babe"

He started massaging my shoulders. I am sure he knew I was nervous. I was always apprehensive whenever "sex" came up.

"Let's not do this?" I pleaded, even though my body yearned for him to rip my clothes off. The last few days I must have fondled myself every night, an act I was experimenting with for the first time. I couldn't understand why suddenly I was so horny all the time.

"Let's not do this," I begged.

"If you insist, but I'm a man, Briana. Men have needs."

I was startled by this comment. I wanted to blurt out the fact that he clearly had forgotten that Christians should not commit fornication, especially the son of a pastor. He was not allowed to use that "men have needs" line with me. But as usual, I kept quiet.

"You know I hate it when you get silent on me," he said.

"This is wrong. We really should not be doing this. I shouldn't even be here. I…" He cut my sentence with a kiss.

"Tell me that you honestly don't feel like you want to have sex with me right now and I will leave you alone." He held me even tighter and started kissing me, this time more heavily. When he released me for air, I was speechless. "Should I take it that your silence means consent?" he laughed and started rubbing my knee, then my thighs once again. My panties were getting wet and I knew I was on the brink of giving it up.

"Can I ask you something?"

"You can ask me anything you like hon?"

"What do you want from me? What do you expect in this relationship?"

"Really Briana?"

"YES, REALLY David."

"First of all I like the fact that you are innocent. That turns me on. You are smart and pretty and you are the type of girl I would be more than happy to introduce to my parents. I need you in my life. You make me happy. I respect whatever decision you make. There is no pressure to have sex, and I am really sorry if that's the impression I gave you just now. I am not just trying to get between your legs but you are just so darn sexy, my hormones can't help but get very active around you at times."

I laughed.

He gathered my hands into his, gazing directly into my eyes. "I love everything about you, and I intend to keep you as my girlfriend for a very long time. You never know what the future holds. If you play your cards right, maybe I will make you into Mrs. Jones."

"Whatever," I said laughing. He then kissed my fingertips one at a time.

I wasn't sure where I wanted my relationship with David to go but his response seemed appropriate.

We sat and talked for hours and about midnight David and I went to bed and ended up "making love" or something close to it. He blew my ear lobe. That didn't turn me on because his breath was kind of tart. He fondled and sucked my breast for less than a minute, then tried to get his penis inside me. I really hadn't gotten wet yet, so he had some problems getting it in. He finally managed but once it was in, he came in less than two minutes. It wasn't what I had imagined, hardly. The foreplay was quick, the actual sex was even quicker and he was out like a light within 30 minutes of having finished. For a man who had been through so many women and had supposedly taken so many virginities, he was totally disappointing. As he slept soundly, I laid there with his head buried in my chest, wondering if things would be better the next time, I sure as hell hoped so.

MAN PROBLEMS

By: Temptress

I must have been on the phone with Mia for about four hours. I listened as she voiced her disgust with men. Her cussing every male species that walked this earth was interspersed with tears from the pain her boyfriend had caused. Apparently, he was cheating on her. I knew she had met a new guy but had been so caught up with my issues I had not kept track of the latest happenings in her social life. She really loved him but was not getting enough in return. I knew better than to give advice because every time I did she ignored it. Mia was a very stubborn person. I realized from early that she had to learn things the hard way.

"You love David, right? So what would you have done if you found out that he was cheating on you?" This question made my stomach churn. I had never really given that much thought. I couldn't imagine David cheating on me. He was too much of a sweetheart, I told myself.

"It depends, Mia," I said in an attempt to answer her question. "I would try to find his reason for cheating then determine whether or not it was something we both could work on. I would analyze the situation as well as our relationship and if I thought he was worth fighting for then I would forgive and give him a second chance. We all make mistakes, but sometimes some of us need a second or third chance to make things right. It all depends on how much you are willing to tolerate just to see if the relationship will work. But then that's me. In the end it boils down to what you want. What does your heart or your gut tells you?" There was this long pregnant pause on the other end of the line.

"Can you give me a minute Mia to take this call?"

"David calling you?"

"Yes."

"Make him wait," Mia said. "Girlfriends come first." We both laughed.

"Hi babe," I said, as I secretly hoped he would not be angry at me for ignoring his calls.

"Didn't you see my several missed calls?"

"I am sorry but…" before I could explain he cut me off. "I bet you are busy with Alex."

"What did you say?"

"Don't play dumb. I know you went to the movie with him. Mia told me."

"So because I went to the movies with him means we are dating?"

"You tell me. I don't see why you thought you had to lie to me about that."

"This is exactly the reason I didn't tell you because you are so jealous. I'd rather avoid your fury and interrogation by not telling you something. Look, I don't have time for this," I shouted before hanging up. I really could not juggle him and Mia right now. I switched back to the line with Mia.

"Why the hell would you tell David I went to the movies with Alex," I screamed into the phone.

"Why are you upset, I didn't think it would be a problem? He mentioned something about you and I going and I just clarified that it was Alex?"

"Was that all Mia because I know you love to talk and David must have asked about Alex?"

"Ummmm…." She paused for a couple minutes and I waited patiently. "Well maybe I told him how you two met…"

"Omg Mia…"

"What, how was I supposed to know? I thought you told David everything that happens in your life. So when I kept spilling information I just assumed he already knew. You two are so close so…."

"Shut up Mia because that is a very poor excuse."

"I am sorry. Why are you so upset about the whole thing though?"

"I have to go. I hope everything works out with you and your guy."

I hung up and screamed into my pillows. It pissed me off sometimes that she just didn't know when to shut up. David and I already had our issues, and I was already tired from constantly fussing with him. I just wished he would do me a favour and end this damn relationship.

ASHAMED!!!!!!!!

By: Temptress

The next day at school seemed to be so tiring. I had long overdue assignments, in addition to our upcoming end of semester exams. The pressure was on. I was still mad with Mia, so I didn't sit beside her as I usually did. After the first hour of lecture, my brain became saturated with information. I grabbed my phone and checked my mentions and direct messages on twitter. Twitter always provided entertainment.

"I am so bored in class…." was the tweet I composed. Mia was the first person to retweet. I ignored her. Two seconds later, I received another mention, also from Mia.

"I am really sorry BRI, this was followed by several sad face smileys."

One minute later a text message came in from David. "I forgot what my baby looks like. Are you so caught up with work and school that you don't think about me anymore?" I wasn't sure how to respond so I waited a few minutes. I went back to twitter and saw another mention from Mia, this time consisting of hugs and kisses.

"You are forgiven," I finally typed, then proceeded to respond to David's message when another text came in.

"What time do you have lunch?" I could bring a barbeque zinger combo with cheese and Pepsi for you?" I could never say no to zinger plus I had not seen David in almost one month

"Sounds good to me; meet me at school for 1pm" I texted back. Mia then came to sit beside me.

"God, when will this lecture end?" Mia said. I slid down my seat in the event the lecturer heard that remark because she could be so tactless at times. I didn't want any unnecessary attention being drawn to me, especially since I hadn't heard a word the lecturer uttered in the last hour.

"Mia, can you stop talking to me, I don't want that woman to direct any questions at me," I whispered.

"So what if she does? Just tell her you don't know." We both laughed.

"I am starving," Mia said. "What are you having for lunch?"

"I am having lunch with D today."

"Oh ok. I won't intrude."

"Yes. I haven't seen him in a while too, so I am looking forward to that," I said.

This was a lie. I wasn't looking forward to anything but the food. It was neither here nor there if I saw D. I was simply going through the motions and doing it because that was what a girlfriend was supposed to do. There was a time when David was the first person I would call during every study/bathroom/snack /TV break I took. He once was my peace of mind from the tedious duties of the world but not anymore. Now, I just wanted to be left alone.

"I need everyone to read chapters 20-25 for tomorrow's lecture." Before she could finish the sentence, students were already rushing out of the class, Mia and I included.

Mia went to buy patties for lunch, while I waited for David at the gazebo. About 10 minutes later he arrived and plopped himself on the seat. I was lost for words as I scrutinized his appearance. What the hell was he thinking showing up to meet me at school like this? He had what seemed like four or five piercings on his left ear and about two on the right, his shirt seemed like a size down from the original size as it fitted just above his navel and to top it all off, his jeans were below his ass, revealing his underpants. I had never been so embarrassed before. I silently hoped none of my friends saw me or decided to be inquisitive. At that moment I wished I could swallow the burger and fries whole. I didn't even know his ears were pierced. I had never seen him in earrings.

"Why did you pierce your ears so many times?"

"Do you like it?"

"Noooo." I shot back without hesitating.

"I think it's sexy," he said smiling.

I was so disgusted. I couldn't even understand why he was smiling, because there was absolutely nothing funny about this.

"I think you need to stop shopping in the kiddies section for clothes." He laughed but I held a straight face. "I usually go a size down. I like when my shirt grips my body; it enhances my muscles."

I shot him a deadly glance. I think less words would be better for him right now because he was really irritating me. I shifted in my seat occasionally ensuring that my back was turned to possible passersby I may know, hoping they wouldn't recognize me from behind.

"So how are you Briana?"

"Stressed from school but ok otherwise," I blurted out, wishing he would hurry with the food and leave. Men were always faster eaters than women. Now would be a great time to prove that. Those six earrings bugged me so much, that I was edging to say something.

"Can you do me a favour please…?" not giving him anytime to respond, "Whenever you are with me, I would really appreciate if you didn't wear six earrings; one is fine, thank you."

"Yes maam," he said smiling. We both finished our meals, and then talked for a short while after. It felt so forced. I didn't feel that connection anymore. There were no more butterflies and, as he leaned to hug and kiss me, the feeling was somehow not mutual. "I love you," he said. Then my automated response came without feeling, without meaning, just a return favour to save his feelings; "I love you too."

"Thanks for lunch," I said placing a gentle kiss on his cheek.

He left, and I headed back to the lecture theatre for a two-hour tutorial.

****

It seemed like 48 hours before that two hour class ended. I felt like a zombie. All I needed was a nice, long, warm bath and my bed to soothe my fatigue. I dragged myself out of class and headed in the direction of the school bus. Without giving my environment much thought, I dragged myself across the pedestrian crossing, desperately yearning to get to a bus. An annoying vehicle wouldn't stop honking its darn horn. I was tired and miserable so the least of things irritated me. A girl then told me someone in the range rover parked to the far left end of the parking lot had been trying to get my attention for the longest while. I gazed in the direction she pointed and realized it was Alex. Just my luck, Lord knows I was drained. I tried to muster all the strength left in my body to get to the vehicle faster.

"You look horrible," Alex said.

"Why, thank you. Good to see you too." I said, rolling my eyes. I climbed in and adjusted the seat.

"I take it that we are heading to my place then?"

"Yeah sure," I said without thought. I had not been back to his house since our little date but we talked over the phone almost every day. I felt comfortable around him.

When I got to his house, he wasted no time. Alex gave me a 20-minute upper body massage. A massage was just what the doctor ordered, because that really helped to relieve the tension I felt. I think I even drifted off to sleep. But what made me slightly uncomfortable was the way he constantly stared at me, focusing on my lips most times. I knew exactly what that meant. Unfortunately, the feeling was mutual but I couldn't. I couldn't cheat on David. As much as I wanted David to end our relationship, it's not like we had broken up as yet. One kiss wouldn't hurt right? Just to see what kissing a more experienced person would be like. David doesn't have to know. I battled with my conscience. He pulled me towards him then rested his hands on my waist.

"I am tempted to kiss you but I am not sure you will allow me to," he said, searching my eyes for answers. My body froze and I felt a lump in my suddenly dry throat and couldn't answer. He leaned forward and kissed me regardless. I kissed back, slowly emerging from my frozen state.

"I am going to teach you how to kiss beautifully," he said a few minutes later. I was a little embarrassed because he was telling me indirectly that I was a terrible kisser.

"Part your lips and work with whatever I do."

I did exactly as he said. He kissed and nibbled on my lips, sucked my tongue leisurely until both our tongues were almost tied-well, that's how it felt to me. I had to ease him off at one point because I was breathless. He was an amazing kisser. His kisses were so leisurely and sensual as his tongue caressed every crevice in my mouth. I could have kissed him all night. At one point, I felt highly aroused. I never felt like this in all the years with David.

I knew something was wrong with the way David kissed me, but I always blamed myself. I figured I was the horrible kisser since I was inexperienced but tonight Alex proved me wrong. When he took me home that night I initiated the kissing before getting out of the vehicle. I was on cloud nine.

NEW BEGINNINGS

By: Bad Bitch

First day on the job and I was already finding customers annoying. They varied from being uptight, obnoxious and very disrespectful, to downright stupid. One woman also nearly made me cuss when she approached and asked if I sold pills? Of course pills are sold here; it is a fucking pharmacy. What amazed me even more was that she actually stood there awaiting a response? I walked away and busied myself with restocking the shelves. I just could not respond to her. So of course she asked for the manager and lodged a complaint about how disrespectful I was. He however apologized to her on my behalf. I don't even know why he did such a thing. Her stupidity needs to go unnoticed. Customers like that I wouldn't care shit about losing. I don't even know why this question bothered me that much. Mr. Williams called me into his office to reprimand me, but before he could get into it, I quickly recited the conversation between the woman and myself. There was no way I was about to be scolded for what was deemed a stupid question. He laughed at the scenario and told me that regardless of how stupid the question was to me, it was my responsibility to address them as best as I could. I knew all this, but just couldn't answer that woman. I could tell that this job was bound to teach me temperance. The staff on the other hand seemed friendly. After all, it was only my first day so I am sure I would see everyone's true personality after a while.

Jemar (by this time we were on first name basis) offered to take me to lunch. Of course, it didn't take much for people to start gossiping but I didn't care. Especially since they thought he would have handled the situation concerning me "disrespecting" the customer a bit differently. Apparently he was a stern person and was often times very harsh on the staff, so his leniency in handling the matter immediately had tongues wagging about how he had eyes for me. Apart from fucking him upon meeting him, I genuinely liked Jemar, so I didn't hesitate to go out with him.

He took me to a nice restaurant for lunch. I could tell he really liked me. We enjoyed the hour and a half lunch break discussing just about any and everything. The ease of our conversations gave me a warm feeling, as if I had known him for a long time. So when he asked me to be his girlfriend on our first real date; I said yes. After all, he had money and earned his wealth the legal way. So this was a good start for me.

Later that day I also met two young ladies by the name of Briana and Melonie. They were regular customers at the pharmacy and would always entertain me whenever they came in. I liked Briana especially. I thought she was cute, sexy and funny. There was something about her that I could not quite pinpoint. She didn't seem like the type who was into women though. Not that I was fully into women either but I wasn't against the idea. Although Budu and I had practiced swinging or I would partake in threesomes, the experience with Bugz and his girlfriend was my first full-on experience with women. With Budu, whatever he wanted, I would give in order to keep him happy. I was his ride or die bitch who suddenly had a change of heart and left him to rot in prison. I later learned the two ladies and Jemar would often times go to karaoke on Tuesdays, so I invited myself to the next one.

Life as a cashier would definitely take some adjustment but my day turned out ok after all. I had a new job, a refined boyfriend and new people in my life.

FANTASY GIRLFRIEND

The strangest thing happened that night. I couldn't stop fantasizing about Briana. There was this uncontrollable desire for a woman I didn't even know. I yearned to hold her naked body next to me that night. Was this my raging hormones or was I suddenly more attracted to women? Oh how I would give anything right now to satisfy my lust for her. I decided to unleash my sexual frustration on my pillows. I nestled one between my legs, as I imagined it being Briana's naked body. I cuddled and kissed the other pillow on which my head rested. This was as close as I would ever get to Briana. As I cuddled, I began to rub myself against the pillow. The feel of the soft pillow grinding against the wet of my vagina turned me on. The more turned on I became the more I humped the pillow pressing harder and harder as I imagined rubbing my naked body against hers, humping her thick sexy thighs while her breasts pressed softly against mine. I was in masturbatory heaven. The more I fantasized about Briana, the more vigorously I dry-humped the pillow. I moaned with pleasure as I imagined her sucking my nipples. We French kissed, squeezed each other's ass and slowly rubbed our pussies against each other. I moaned even louder and screamed her name. My groin ached with pleasure as I rubbed furiously against the pillow. What if my mother overheard all my moaning, the bed springs squeaking and caught me in the middle of my sordid pillow fucking session? Not to mention hearing me scream a girl's name? What would my Christian mother think? It was bad enough that I was already fornicating but to be bisexual, I am sure she would have crucified me.

For a brief moment I wondered if I was a pervert. I was slightly disgusted by myself but also strangely turned on by it. I humped the pillow even more frantically now, keen to get the maximum possible pleasure. I threw my head back and screamed Briana's name one last time as I gave birth to a magnificent orgasm. I snuggled closer to my pillow girlfriend, gripping her and gently kissed her once more before falling asleep.

The next morning I woke up startled when I realized the compromising position I was in. I wondered if my mother had walked into my room at all that morning. She had a tendency to look in on me, especially when I slept for more than the conventional eight hours.

I quickly withdrew the pillow from between my legs and began re arranging them. It was then I noticed my pillow was a little damp with remnants of my pussy juice from my session the night before.

Still remembering the ecstasy I experienced the night before, I buried my face into the damp patch and sniffed my juices; it turned me on. I fondled my clitoris as I dabbed my face in it, licking and making it moist as I imagined it was Briana's pussy. "Kimberly, you will be late for work if you don't get out of bed this minute," my mother shouted as she approached my room. I pulled my hands from my crotch just in time for the door to open. "I am up. I am about to take a shower," I responded. "Ok. Don't let me come back in here," she said closing the door. I was so frightened about almost being caught masturbating as well as a little annoyed that my session was interrupted. My heart raced with the thrill of what just occurred.

FULL DISCLOSURE

The next day at work I had an actual conversation with my fantasy girlfriend from last night. We had more than just a conversation. We had lunch together, though this was accidental. It just so happened that the table she occupied in Burger King was the only one with a vacant seat. So I asked politely to join her. "You are the new cashier at the pharmacy right?" she asked. "Yes. My name is Kimberly." I said. "Sorry I didn't mean anything by it. I am Briana," she said. I smiled. I knew who you were. If only you knew how I raped you in my dreams last night, I thought. She then asked about the job. We talked about what each of us liked to do for fun after which I mentioned karaoke tonight. She burst my bubble by saying she wouldn't be able to make it. I felt crushed. I didn't mind having her as a friend though because she had a really warm personality. So when she offered to exchange numbers this made me happy. I enjoyed our brief conversation. Her lunch break ended half hour before mine, so I was eventually left to finish lunch alone.

This wasn't for long as an old friend by the name of Candy decided to join me. She still had that lovely booty. I had not seen her in quite a while. "Hey girl, how are you? How is Budu? You two haven't visited me in ages"

I was surprised by her question. Clearly she was not aware of the ordeal. I thought the whole world would have known by now. "Budu and I split," I said not wanting to provide details.

"Oh wow. You two seemed inseparable. I am sorry to hear that," she said.

"Yeah, shit happens," I responded.

"So are you still making that ass clap," I asked.

She laughed. "You know that's how I make my change. I aint got rich men flocking me like you do so I gotta hustle," she said rubbing her hands together.

Candy was an exotic dancer. One of the best I had known. This girl had expertise when it came to dancing on a pole and did the wildest and freakiest of things. She was also the third person in one of my ménage a trois with Budu. I remember vividly the night Budu had taken us to dinner. After several rounds of Patron, vodka and gin, our voices became softer, almost a whisper and we were forced to lean in closer to hear each other. I also noticed that there was a tingle in my pussy. After completing our meals, I excused myself to the ladies room and the door had barely closed, when it flung back open to allow Candy to enter. She said the liquor had gotten to her too and figured since women always go to the bathroom in twos, she would join me. The liquor must have gotten to me too because I accepted her explanation at face value and continued on my mission of the moment relief. She came out of the stall as I washed my hands and checked my makeup, slid behind me and whispered in my ear that she wanted me for dessert. I was shocked! I stood dumbstruck as I thought of something to say. Pulling me around, she gently kissed me on the lips. Still I remained speechless. Interpreting my silence as consent, Candy kissed me again, this time softly running her tongue all over my lips. Without any thought I parted my lips and accepted her proffered tongue. That was when she organized the ménage a trois with Budu. I must say I was nervous at first but enjoyed it. Maybe I should show up at the strip club later and watch Candy in action. After all, the main reason I had planned to go to karaoke was to see Briana, and she wasn't going to be there.

Candy and I chit chatted and brought each other up to date on our lives until my lunch break was over. Her lifestyle had not changed much but I was glad things were still working out for her. We exchanged numbers.

CLUB LEVITATE

That night I visited club Levitate as planned but Jemar accompanied me. This was my favourite adult club not only because Candy worked there but also because they had a great variety of excellent quality strippers. Jemar's enthusiasm was very entertaining as he claimed to love me even more now that he realized I was more sexually liberated.

Tuesday night's show consisted of women performing tricks that were sometimes unheard of. The first performer wasted no time, removing her clothes, as she stepped onto the stage. No form of teasing. I wasn't a professional dancer but I knew you were supposed to slowly and seductively remove your clothes, leaving the area the audience eagerly anticipated for last. This girl did the total opposite. The first thing to come off was her g- string. However, she had a nice, smooth, plump ass. In a matter of seconds, she was totally nude. After that, she flicked backwards then maintained a crab like position before opening her legs to give us a good view of her well shaved pussy. Then to my disbelief, her pussy lips parted and a small white ping pong ball popped out. There was uproar in the audience. I had never seen anything like that in all my years of watching exotic dancers. What she lacked in undress skills, she made up for in other areas. The audience applauded again and two more balls popped out. This was fucking unbelievable. She then laid on her back, opened her legs again then placed a cigarette between her pussy lips which she asked a man from the audience to light. I watched as she took several deep breaths while squinting her pussy, holding the cigarette in place after which she removed it and blew a cloud of smoke out of her pussy. This she repeated several times and on each occasion the smoke became thicker. The audience was in a frenzy once more and a last ping pong ball shot out that was bigger than the other two. This completed her performance and the men sitting directly by the stage started cheering "pocket pussy, pocket pussy." Soon the whole club was shouting 'pocket pussy', Jemar and I included. It was simply amazing.

The host presented herself onstage with Pocket Pussy and announced they were about to play a game. She needed three men to come onstage to strip and entertain the now very popular dancer. The winner would receive a full body sexual satisfaction. Whatever that entailed, the men went crazy. It was such a sad sight to see them tripping over each other to get to the stage. Pussy was a hell of a weakness for some men. The first contestant didn't look more than 19 years of age and still had his boyish looks. He introduced himself as 'Swiper'. . Jemar and I laughed. "Momma's boy" a man shouted from the back of the club. "Isn't it past your bedtime?" he continued. "You can't handle Pocket Pussy," another man shouted. The host asked them to be quiet.

Pocket Pussy then took the microphone and said, "Besides I don't mind a young cock, isn't that right ladies?" The audience cheered in agreement. The young fellow danced up a storm and wasn't bad at all. His waistline seemed boneless as he twisted and conformed into various positions effortlessly. When he finally took his clothes off, he stood motionless with his well erect cock. The women cheered him on. Some of them grabbed their breasts, lifted their tops exposing themselves to Swiper. The boy became more excited, as his cock made little twitches. Pocket Pussy cupped his balls and let her hands run slowly along his shaft. This was apparently too much and the poor lad bent over, screamed and ejaculated over his hands, semen dripping between his fingers. I felt so embarrassed for the young man. He grabbed his clothes and rushed off the stage while some of the men in the audience laughed uncontrollably. Jemar placed his hands on his forehead. I supposed he felt slightly humiliated. The second contestant introduced himself as 'Big Daddy'. He was 52-years-old and there was nothing entertaining about the performance. His movements were not in sync with the rhythm of the music, as he seemed to be in his own little world. When he finally decided to grace us with his nakedness, he had no erection. Instead, I saw a long limp penis, flagging with soggy balls that looked like a bag of earthworms.

"I can't watch any more of this Kim. Let's go home please," Jemar said. I wasn't entertained either but I wanted to see how the competition would unfold, not to mention my burning desire to see my Candy in action. Jemar was intruding.

"I am sorry dear but you don't match my requirements. Thank you nevertheless for your effort, applause please?" said Pocket Pussy. "Babe, let's go," Jemar said, pulling me towards the door. I so wanted to stay and watch but didn't want to upset my boyfriend so I went along reluctantly.

BONDS BROKEN

By: Temptress

Fortunately, I had no lectures on Wednesdays because I don't know how I would have managed especially since I had a hard time censoring the strong sexual images that pervaded my mind. My thoughts strayed from just a kiss with Alex to doing and telling him naughty things. My mood was perfect for work this evening though, I could handle even the most miserable of patients.

The sound of the message alert sent me rushing to check my cell phone which showed an invite from Mia: "Dinner and movies at my house tonight?"

"Sure but make it 8. I get off at 7," I responded. "Ok, see you then," she replied a few seconds later followed by her usual smiley face emoji.

I rushed to the kitchen and rummaged through the refrigerator and cupboards like a scavenger. I had forgotten to buy groceries. I stumbled over a can of sausages and half of a bread decorated with mildew. I took out two slices, scraped the mildew off, applied my butter, slit my sausages and laid each piece uniformly on the bread. I then cut another slice of the bread. This one seemed more edible so I placed it on top of my sausages to complete the sandwich. This was complemented by a long glass of ice water, more than enough to satisfy me until work. I glanced at the clock.

It was almost nine. I needed to be out the house in half hour or I would be late. I grabbed my towel and headed towards the shower when my cell phone rang.

"Hi baby, how are you?"

"Wow you are happy?" David said letting out a deep long sigh.

"And I see you are depressed. What's with the sighing?"

"O God, Umm…" then he sighed again. By this time I was frozen in my tracks. My mind raced at 2,000 miles per hour.

"David, what happened?" He sighed once more.

"Remember I told you I stopped by Mia's house the other day…."

"Yes I remember." Then there was a long pause.

"Well, I have been spending a little more time than usual with her. I….sort of…I sort of… Bri I am so sorry. I really didn't mean to hurt you."

"You sort of what…" I shouted in the phone. I knew the answer but wanted to hear him say it.

"I kissed her. I have been messing around with her." I felt like someone stabbed me in the chest with a knife. How could I not have suspected something between them?

How could Mia do that?

"I am so sorry but you have been so busy with school. We hardly see each other. We don't talk long hours anym…"

"So that gives you the right to cheat with my best friend?"

"I am so sorry Briana. Please for…"

"Why are you telling me this now?"

"It's tearing me apart that I cheated on you and I just wanted to clear my conscience and start over with you before it's too late. I wanted you to hear the whole story in the event Mia tries to tell you otherwise"

"Ok," the only words I managed to mutter in my broken state. I never imagined being cheated on. It's not even the fact that he cheated that killed me but the fact that the other girl was MIA…MY MIA…MY BEST FRIEND. Who does that? How could he even think of doing that then have the audacity to use "I am busy with school" to justify his infidelity. I had nothing to say to him, although I was just as guilty because I had kissed Alex, but that happened only once. My situation was different. Wasn't it? Even though we had our issues, I had continued to respect the little that was left of our relationship. This I could never forgive; an affair with my best friend because I was busy, a fucking affair with my fucking best friend? This was unbelievable.

"Briana, say something. I am really sorry."

"We are done David. Have a nice life." I ended the call and dragged myself to the bathroom still trying to digest all that I had just heard. I lay still in the empty bathtub for about half hour trying to cement the details in my head. All this time when she was having problems with her guy....that was David? How long had this been going on? How did this affair even start? Is that why she told him I went to the movies with Alex? Was that her attempt to break us up? Did he love her? I had an instant headache trying to answer all these questions.

I had wanted to break up with David for some time, but had no reason to because he was still performing all his boyfriend duties. Now he had messed up, and I planned to use this to my advantage.

The phone rang about 15 times since I hung up. They were all from David. There was nothing he could possibly say that would change my mind. There were no tears, just anger; anger at Mia and David. I felt betrayed.

"Bloop bloop" a text came in from David which read "So that's how it is. You are just going to leave? Just like that? You are willing to toss our three years of relationship out the window like it never existed? I know that's what you always wanted. You can run along to Alex, you pompous bitch. How could you?"

Is David serious right now? Pompous bitch...wasn't sure what that meant, but it was the first time anyone had called me a bitch. I blocked his number immediately. Mia was next on my list. I would still see her later. I just wasn't sure how I would handle the matter but needed to hear her side.

I was officially running behind schedule for work. I showered quickly, got dressed then left. My phone rang and I let it go to voice mail. It rang again, once, twice, thrice, before I looked at the caller ID, it was Alex. I still wasn't in the mood to talk. Besides, I wasn't particularly fond of men at this moment, so Alex was the last person I wanted to hear from.

Mia texted me the whole day at work, and I made sure to respond to each one. I even reassured her that her movie date was still on. Coming to work was the best thing that happened to me that day. The patients somehow cheered me up with their witty remarks. Alex also texted and called the whole day, but I ignored him as well.

By the time I was due for lunch break, I had no appetite. I worked like never before only pausing for bathroom breaks. I needed to remain busy at all times in order to forget about this morning's event and was not about to break down at work. Last thing I needed was co-workers in my business. I worked and worked and worked even more. When there were no more patients registered to see the doc, I busied myself with paperwork, sterilizing equipment and just about everything else I could find to occupy myself with. I worked until the clock struck 7 then was out the door. Not a minute later than 7.

I took deep breaths and braced myself for the worst the moment I approached Mia's driveway. "Hi Bri," she said throwing her arms around me hugging me tightly. "So glad you could make it."

"Of course, I need this. Girls' night," I said. We ordered pizza and watched Tyler Perry's Single Moms Club. The movie was interrupted by Mia's cell phone ringing. She looked at the caller then glanced at me. "Is your phone off Bri?"

"No. Why?"

"David is calling me and he only does that whenever he is unable to reach you."

"Mmm," I said. How could she lie so blatantly? She was very convincing too.

"Did you two have a quarrel? Should I answer this call because you know he is going to ask for you or if I have spoken to you? What should I say to him?"

I shrugged my shoulders and continued to watch the movie.

I watched her every move through the corners of my eyes as she answered the call. Her body language changed drastically, somewhat stiff. At one point I wasn't sure if she was even breathing. He must have told her about this morning. With my eyes fixed on the television and a forced smile as if I was enjoying the show, I watched as she tried earnestly to analyze me. I was being a damn good hypocrite tonight. Something she had been doing with me for Lord knows how long. When she hung up, she was so nervous I swore I heard her swallow her Adam's apple.

I glanced at her and she literally froze.

"You look tense Mia. Come, sit and finish watching the movie with me?"

She stared at me and remained frozen in position. Not sure if she thought I was going to fight her. I couldn't hurt a fly but I felt some kind of way knowing that she felt intimated by me. It was a good feeling really.

"Bri.. I am sorry. I was going to tell you but I didn't know how. I am really sorry." I gently slapped the couch beside me beckoning her to come and sit.

"I am not going to hurt you." I said laughing. She forced a smile then finally came and sat beside me.

"I just have one question, Why David?"

She looked at her feet before answering. "I don't know. I let my emotions get the best of me I guess. I am really, really, really sorry. I had planned to stop but…but…I just didn't think he would volunteer to tell you something like this. I am really sorry"

"Did you have sex?"

"Nooooo. We only kissed. That's it. I swear."

"Ok." I said. I didn't want to know the details anymore. I didn't care how long or when it started. I was done with them both. I got up and headed to the bathroom.

I stared into the mirror for a brief moment until the devil gave me a bright idea. This is what you get, you lying, conniving bitch, I thought as I pulled Mia's toothbrush out of its holder on the counter. I knelt in front of the toilet and dipped the brush in the water and swirled it around. "Oh my, oh my," I said entertaining myself as I swirled around even faster. "Oh my, is that a stain? Shame on me. I scrubbed the stains from every corner of the toilet bowl with the toothbrush until the bowl nearly sparkled. "There, the toilet is as good as new," I said replacing the tooth brush in the holder. I washed my hands then headed back to the living room, grabbed my belongings and headed toward the door.

"That's it. You are not going to scream at me or punch me in the face or anything." I ignored her and proceeded to let myself out.

"Bri, can you please say something." I continued to ignore her. "Are we still friends." I paused before closing the grill behind me.

"No we are not friends. We never were friends. Best friends don't throw themselves at each other's boyfriends. Don't fucking call or talk to me ever again. Not in this life time." I closed the grill then headed up the road without looking back. Tears welled up in my eyes but I fought them

A few tears managed to escape when I was in the taxi. But the moment I was behind closed doors in the comfort of my home, my world crumbled. Reality hit hard. All the events replayed. I cried, I heaved, I cried until it felt as if every ounce of fluid in my body was gone. I cried until I was no longer able to produce a sound. I cried until my eyes were swollen and my whole body convulsed. I cried until my own tears became my lullaby. I cried until I slept.

A SURPRISING COMFORT

Forty-eight hours had passed and I remained listless on the floor in my bedroom. I was desperately in need of a shower and food but didn't have the willpower. Instead, my appetite was satiated with hurt and betrayal. There was no more Mia or David. How does someone lose both their best friend and boyfriend at once? How can your boyfriend even decide to have a fling with your best friend? I just couldn't understand it no matter how many times I replayed the events. I looked at my cell phone and saw about 40 missed calls; 10 from Mia, 20 from Alex and the other 10 were from a private number but I assumed they were all from David. I tried so hard to compose myself, but it was just so hard. Laying in the same spot on the floor, and drowning in my sorrows was way easier to do. I drifted in and out of sleep.

Very loud banging on my door disturbed my slumber a few minutes later. I remained quiet. There came a second then a third knock but I still remained quiet. There was a brief moment of silence. I listened keenly for anything that would help me to figure out who had the nerve to be at my door. I swear I was ready to use my ratchet if Mia or David was audacious enough to show up. My cell phone then rang sounding louder than usual. I grabbed it quickly and placed it on silent. There was a fourth knock on the door, "I know you are there, I heard your phone ringing. Briana let me in." That was Alex's voice. What the hell was he doing here? He had no right to show up at my house unannounced. "If I did something to you can you please let me know. I hate being ignored. Briana open the damn door." I didn't even understand why he was getting upset. I got up feebly, approached the door and garnered the little energy I had left to open it. Alex looked at me as if he had seen a ghost. He stepped past me then closed the door. Next thing I knew, I was off the floor and in his arms as he chauffeured me around my one-bedroom apartment as if he had been there before. He placed me on the bed then headed in the direction of the kitchen. I listened to his every move as he opened my cupboards, drawers, refrigerator and even the oven. I felt embarrassed because I knew everything he touched was empty. There must have been only a single bottle of water in the refrigerator.

"Hi, I would like to order a large pepperoni pizza with cheese, pineapple, cinnamon and cheese sticks with a 12-oz soda." I heard the footsteps coming towards me. "Bri, what's your address?" I wanted to say something witty or asked why he assumed I ate pork but didn't bother, "6 Paddington Terrace." He then left the room, heading towards the bathroom. A few seconds later I heard water running in the bath. He returned and attempted to undress me. "What are you doing?" I said, slapping his hands. "When was the last time you showered or ate?" Embarrassed by the question, I held my head down. He attempted to undress me once more. I shifted. "I can do it myself." I said. "Really, go ahead then." He stood there watching me.

Who was I kidding? I could barely manage to open the door much less to undo jeans and blouse buttons. My vision was blurry, I felt light headed and unusually weak but if I allowed him to undress me he would see me naked and I didn't want that.

"I won't do anything to you if that's what you are worried about. Besides I like my women well fed, alert, energized and responsive, all of which you are not right now." That was a bit harsh I thought but it was the truth; I was a mess. He undressed me, lifted me, took me to the bathroom and placed me in the warm tub of soapy water. He touched me innocently, washing every crevice and curve on my body. I felt like a child all over again. The last time I had someone bathe me was at age eight. All this he did without uttering a word and I just stared at him. He dried my skin, wrapped me in a towel and took me back to the room. Without asking any questions, he pulled out all the drawers until he discovered the one with my underwear.

"What type of foods don't you eat?" What a question I thought but answered regardless. This was a very awkward time to get to know me. He dressed me, put money on the bedside table for the pizza and left without even saying a word. I didn't even get to thank him.

Shortly after the delivery guy arrived. The food smelled very good. I couldn't wait to sink my teeth in a slice of pizza. I devoured the food like I had not eaten for months. For every bite of food I took, I chewed twice then swallowed. At one point I stuffed my mouth with everything – the pizza, cheese sticks and cinnamon sticks. I felt so hungry all of a sudden. I ate until I let out the loudest and most vulgar burp. This minute I was starved then the next minute my tummy was so full, I could hardly walk. I must have dozed off for about one hour when I heard a knock at the door. Feeling revived, I jumped up and rushed to the door.

"You look much better. Come and help me with the bags" Alex said, heading towards the vehicle. I brought in almost two dozen bags. I couldn't believe my eyes. Alex had gone grocery shopping. That explained why he asked me what I didn't eat but I was too tired and hungry to even put the pieces together. I felt a little embarrassed knowing that it was his first time at my house and he had found me in such a distressing situation. Interestingly, he still had not asked what was wrong but continued to care for me. I really appreciated this. He ate the two slices of pizza I left and the remnants of cheese bread while I unpacked. The more I unpacked, the more I wanted to jump on Alex and tell him thanks. He basically bought everything I needed, enough to serve for a month or two. I spun around, grabbed him and said thanks.

"No problem dear. I am glad you look like yourself once again. I am going to leave now," he said.

"So soon?" I really wanted him to stay.

"I have a meeting," he said, heading for the door.

"Wait Alex," I paused. "Aren't you going to ask me what's wrong?"

"No...You will tell me when you are ready. Later Bri...".

I watched as he got into the vehicle and drove off.

A SECOND CHANCE

By: Bad Bitch

Work got easier now that I was settled. A few of the women continued to despise me after failing miserably to capture Jemar's interest. It was no longer a secret that we were together. I never showed any form of intimacy towards him at work but this still made them jealous. It didn't faze me as I was getting my money and that was all that mattered. I had my hair and nails done routinely but whenever it came to shopping, Jemar held back on the funds. Until I learned how to let go of brand name clothing, he would not buy me anything. He didn't believe in that. His theory was once something looked good and fit accordingly then you should get it. As, for me, it could be as ugly as a scarecrow, once it was a brand, I was buying it. Brands lasted way longer than the cheaper stuff. That was my theory.

Jemar also encouraged me to go back to school to pursue Mathematics and English Language. I told him I couldn't do the school thing. I was never disciplined enough to study and attend classes. After realizing he was not listening to any of my petty reasons, I decided to use money as the issue. I told him I didn't want to share my already small salary to pay for my tuition and books and he offered to cover the cost. He insisted so I told him I would give it a try. I guess this was the second chance at life that I prayed for, so might as well make the most of it.

Briana and I had also been corresponding more often. We even went to a few parties together. I was right about her. She was a cool person to be around. Maybe I could ask her to help me with my studies. She was very smart and I admired the fact that she was able to work long hours, do well in school, live on her own, manage the bills and other expenses plus be a good girlfriend. I don't think I could succeed at all that at once. These were all qualities I wished to possess someday.

Jemar was a decent guy, but sometimes I felt he was just too nice for me. He said the right things, treated me like a lady, apologized, admitted when he was wrong, made an attempt to work out all our issues, earned his money legally and respected women. I don't know, he was just too nice. I had gotten used to the aggression, drugs and occasional slaps in the face when I answered back. Not that I missed it, but I was just not used to all this niceness. Everything seemed to be going right but I still wasn't sure I was happy. Maybe I didn't truly know what I wanted. I had asked for a second chance to do things differently in life but now I kind of missed my old, get- rich- quick life. This new life took time, patience and determination-all of which I lacked.

I LIKE ADVENTURE

By: Temptress

I decided to skip school for the rest of this week. I wasn't missing much with the classes because those lecturers read the contents of their slides word for word. It was more practical to do my own reading while awaiting the lecture notes to be uploaded to the student portal. I was also trying to avoid Mia. It's not only that I would avoid school more than usual because I hated Mia, but I just wasn't ready to go back. Instead, I worked longer hours at the medical centre.

I never officially told Alex he was my boyfriend but in my head he was. Although we conversed on a more regular basis than we used to, I still had not gotten around to telling him what had happened with David and I, and he didn't ask. I knew he must have figured that out somehow because prior to this I was always apprehensive about going out with him or I would make references to my "boyfriend" in almost every conversation and was no longer doing any of that. If he wanted to see me I was always available. I liked Alex, and he was doing and saying all the right things, so I was willing to work with whatever we had in the making.

A group of girls from work were planning on visiting club Levitate at the end of tonight's shift. I had never been to a strip club or even had any interest in that sort of thing, but the adventure of it appealed to me. According to the girls, the club's theme for tonight was FREAKY FRIDAY, this piqued my interest.

****

The action had already begun by the time we got to the club. Live sex on stage was the highlight. Kim and Melonie were the first to get excited by the action. I could tell they were regulars. I, on the other hand, was trying to appear to be accustomed to seeing all this excitement. I watched as nude girls pranced around on stage, extending their legs at a 360 degree angle to the audience. Men and women whistled, cheered, while some even threw money at them. I watched as one guy neatly rolled what looked like a one hundred dollar bill and shoved it into the stripper's vagina. She continued to dance as if nothing happened. One girl grabbed the tongue of another with her teeth before sucking like she was enjoying a dick. The other woman finally pulled the money out of her vagina then turned to face the two women kissing intensely.

"Fuck Candy's pussy" I heard a man shout.

"Get in there Delicious" shouted Kim and Melonie. I was catching on. My eyes darted swiftly around the club, scanning everyone and everything, photographically grasping bits and pieces of information. Thus far, I gathered that the girl on the floor with legs apart was Candy and one of the girls kissing was Delicious. I wondered how they came up with those stage names. Now Delicious and the other girl were staring into Candy's open legs. Delicious went in, fucking Candy slowly, pushing and pulling them in and out of her vagina as if trying to accomplish a goal. The other girl leaned in, kissed Candy's pussy and sucked on her clit as Delicious forced her hand deeper and deeper inside until her thumb slipped in easily. She carefully pulled her fingers together and balled them up inside Candy fucking her deeply with her fist. Candy squirmed on the stage and let out a scream. By now my throat was dry. The live action made me slightly uncomfortable; yet, my eyes were still glued to the stage. Delicious then climbed onto Candy's mouth silencing her moans. Delicious was fucking her face like a champion rodeo rider. Next, Candy pushed her pelvis upward and gave birth to an orgasm that pushed the other girl's fist out of her body, along with a flood of orgasmic juices. Her body arched and jerked as she continued to spew juice. By this time, the stage was flooded with thousand dollar bills. That was intense, I thought.

"I would like a private session with Candy," Kim said with lust in her eyes. The girls then headed to a room towards the back of the building, as another set of girls came onstage. This set was semi nude, sporting a bra and thong. "Ladies this is where I leave you," Kim said. Smiling, Melonie said "You just could not resist a private session huh."

"No. You know Candy is my favourite." She then turned to me and asked "Are you up for more adventure Briana? The look in Kim's eyes told me she was up to no good, but I was curious to see more. "Sure," I answered. Melonie looked surprised. "Well I will be right here when you two get back," she said.

I followed Kim as we entered a dark room in which I could make out a bed and two chairs. I sat on the chair and looked around. "You seem tense," Kim said. "You don't have to do anything you are not comfortable with," she reassured me. "Have you ever had your pussy sucked by a woman...better yet have you ever had it done at all?" I didn't answer, just smirked, leaving her to wonder. I wasn't into women, so the thought of a woman having her mouth on my vagina had never crossed my mind, just like being here was also a first and I wasn't sure what the hell I was getting into.

A few minutes later Candy entered the room and closed the door. "We have company tonight? That's going to be three grand extra," she said peering over at me. "Not this time. She's a virgin, so I am just showing her a thing or two," Kim said. Candy face lit up with a cunning smile as she stared at me, which made me feel very awkward. "Kim, do you remember your first time in the bathroom that night?" she said. Stopping just short of touching me, Candy unbuttoned her shirt and jiggled her double D size boobs in my face.

I think I had stopped breathing the whole time she was over me. Candy threw herself on the ground and crawled to Kim. "I am your whore, use me," she said, sticking her fingers under her underwear and rubbing her pussy. "Use me," she repeated, finger fucking herself. I could hear Kim breathing heavily and watched as she unzipped her shorts and removed her underwear. "Bring your fat ass over here bitch," she said, grabbing Candy by the hair. Kim squatted, covering Candy's lips with her black, hairy vagina. Like an expert artist at work, the stripper used her tongue to expertly explore Kim's crevices before settling on the moist, pink clitoris. Flicking her 'brush' with expertise and seeing the pleasure Kim was obviously enjoying, I began to get horny watching the two women. I had this sudden desire to feel a tongue traversing my pussy. I had this desire to strip, fondle myself and have the time of my life with them but fought the urge. I am a nurse, well not yet certified but I was only about a few months away from achieving that and had a reputation to maintain, I told myself. I can't do this.

"Stick out your tongue," Kim said and as Candy complied, lying flat on her back, I watched in amazement as she rode that tongue like a dick, bouncing her clit even harder against Candy's mouth. Kim looked like she was about to explode. By now my underwear was soaking wet. Candy then placed her fingers deep inside her pussy as Kim came hard, pissed all over her face and chest. I was suddenly nauseous, wanting desperately to make a run for it but a mix of curiosity and excitement kept me bound to the chair. Sitting up, Candy collected some of the golden shower in her mouth, swallowing hard to enjoy what she got as much as possible. Closing my eyes in a bid to block this last image, I looked up again to see that while they had change positions, the intensity of the women's action had not lessened. Kim shoved two fingers up Candy's ass and a few seconds later added two more.

With four fingers plunging rapidly and deeply inside her ass, Kim gyrated rapidly on Candy's pussy. "Fuck, I am gonna cum" Candy screamed, followed a few seconds by Kim who shuddered astride her as the ride came to an end. Kim then slipped her fingers out of Candy's ass and fed them to her. Candy sucked greedily, moaning, basking in orgasmic shock. I couldn't tolerate anymore.

I dashed out of the room and into the ladies room. I vomited until my entire body felt dry. The image of Candy basically eating her own shit and swallowing someone's pee made me vomit. I vomited until I was unable to bring up anything but bile. I vomited until my chest hurt. That was the nastiest thing I had ever seen. I felt like I had just booked myself on a first class flight to hell.

How could Kim find it pleasurable to pee in someone's mouth? I was curious to know how much she paid Candy for that freaky encounter. I just could not believe what had happened. These women basically let you do anything to them once you were spending. My mouth felt very nasty after I had finally finished vomiting. Luckily, I always had a small bottle of Listerine and a mint in my cosmetic bag. I immediately headed back to Melonie, grabbed my purse then returned to the ladies room. I wasn't in the mood for any more freaky encounters. I had seen enough.

I didn't want to seem rude by leaving so abruptly. After all, I had come with the girls so I decided to spend half hour more. I headed back to sit with Melonie and watched a few more performances. Half hour passed and there was still no sign of Kim. I hugged Melonie before I left. Freaky Friday had more than lived up to its billing as far as I was concerned.

BURIED ALL THE LOVE

I spent the next few days officially clearing David and Mia out of my system. I continued to ignore phone calls and text messages from both. They now had the chance to officially be together, so I hoped they would be happy. I hated them, especially David. I was not ok. It ripped me apart every time I replayed the incident. I missed my best friend but things had to stay this way.

Alex was my rebound guy now that David was gone, and he adjusted to the role wonderfully. I was happy with him. Next weekend we would travel out of town and spend the entire time at a resort. This would be our first official time together and I was excited. I was still amazed by the way he handled the situation with me withdrawing from the world for 48 hours. He was so concerned. I was really appreciative and admired him even more. I didn't know if I could ever again love anyone the way I loved David, especially with this new found anger I had towards men. Still, I was willing to give Alex a try.

As for Kim, she was more than a bit on the wild side but I try not to judge people. She entertained my curiosity and I had learnt a great deal from her. She was actually not a bad person to have in my life but I wasn't sure I could love her like a best friend and I think that's what she wanted. Either that or she was bisexual. It was wrong to assume but her demeanour sometimes suggested otherwise. I didn't know how to bring that up in a conversation either without feeling awkward, so instead, I made sure to come across as being addicted strictly to dicks and hoped that in the long run she would lose any sexual interest in me.

This was now my new social life in a nutshell. More frequent outings with Kim and a few people from work as well as more time spent with Alex, my rebound boyfriend.

A PLEASANT SURPRISE

By: Bad Bitch

With all that Jemar had been doing for me I decided to up my girlfriend game a notch. I wanted to show him that I was grateful for everything he had done by preparing my best version of a five course meal. I showered and changed into lingerie the moment he called to say he was half hour from home.

I greeted him at the door in a mere thong with a thin, sheer dress thrown over it. The smell of food wafted through the apartment the minute he entered. A very pleased yet cunning smirk was plastered on his face as he entered, taking a few minutes to sum up the situation. "What are we celebrating dear?"

"Just a token of my love and appreciation for you, my dear," I responded, with a broad smile on my face. I planted light kisses on his lips, prompting him to grab and squeeze my exposed ass, at which point I stopped him. "You can have me for dessert," I teased. "Come this way please," I said, leading him to the dining table. First on the menu was grilled shrimp followed by a classic Italian salad. I prepared the bread for the salad into bite sized pieces with tomatoes, cucumbers, onions, tossed with a combination of fresh herbs and just enough vinegar and oil to give them a nice gloss. I watched him eat with gusto, as he anticipated the main course which was Mediterranean pasta followed by chicken steak mixed with spinach, green beans, baby carrots drizzled with mushroom sauce with a serving of rice. I knew nothing about baking, so I completed the course with the left over cheese cake from Pastry Passion. I was happy with the look of satisfaction on Jemar's face. He flung his head back, unbuttoned his shirt, unbuckled his pants and stripped down to his underpants and merino. It was my first time cooking for him, and he had enjoyed it. Funny enough my mother had to beg me to help in the kitchen at home, but I was always more than happy to cook for a man, at least the men I cared about. I cleaned up the kitchen, giving him ample time to shower and prepare for part two of my presentation.

Laying on the bed with legs wide open, I eagerly anticipated the end of his shower. I was so aroused my clit was already swollen and protruded above the folds of my labia. Coming out of the bathroom, he dove hungrily unto the bed, his head finding its way between my legs, lips expertly settling around my clit. The wet suction pulsed in rhythm, stretching my clit then releasing it as I moaned in tandem with each motion. He took a longer, deeper draw on my erect clit, pulling it extra hard and extra-long, between his wet lips. Every nerve ending in my body seemed to stand on end. I nearly levitated. I arched my back and cried out. There was no escaping this sensation.

Sensing that I was ready to be taken, Jemar then slowly and gently slid his swollen, throbbing cock inside me and at first the pain seemed more than I could bear but as he continued to thrust rhythmically inside me, pleasure began to override the hurt. With expert timing he spread my legs wider, forcing me to take deep breaths as I felt my pussy split open to accommodate even more of his rock hard cock. Pinned against the mattress, I was being pounded by the full force of Jemar's cock but my body wasn't complaining. Rather, it seemed to be rejoicing at this welcomed invasion. Impossible as it seemed, I tried to spread my legs even more as he pinned my hips firmly to the bed, pressing himself more deeply into my swollenness, releasing his cum inside me. For the first time since Budu I felt a connection. It was not just sex. We cuddled and slept in each other's arms for the rest of the night.

CEMENTING MYSELF

With the new academic year, I now had a different schedule. I worked mainly the morning shift and attended classes in the evening. I had the support of Jemar and that was all that mattered. Fortunately, I also had Briana assisting me with assignments occasionally. It had only been one month into my course, but I felt like quitting already. School was hard. Maths was difficult but English Language seemed more manageable. I couldn't believe they wanted to give me a test in the first month of our course. No matter the outcome, I was proud of myself for pushing myself to do things that I never did before. I reworked a few of the practice questions I received in class, I altered the numbers and equations, I worked past examination papers and felt exceptionally proud because, I was actually understanding different concepts. I spent the whole evening studying, only taking breaks to eat and check up on my beau and Bri. Bri also had several well overdue assignments, so she too was buried with work.

Bugz had been calling me all day, but I ignored him. We hadn't spoken since the party, because I thought it best to avoid him completely. Money and material things were my weaknesses. They always were, and it didn't take much for me to be mesmerized by the thought of being able to get what I wanted when I wanted it. I could not bring myself to say no to certain people and things, so avoiding him was best. Bugz was a constant reminder of my old life and I knew he could drag me back down in the wink of an eye. I told my mother to say I was busy and would call back but never returned any of his calls. I knew time was running out for me, because he was likely to show up without warning if I continued to ignore him.

I chose to ignore the call when a private number came up. I wondered if this was a ploy by Bugz to reach me. It rang again and again, so I decided to answer and give an excuse about being busy. "My ride or die bitch" the voice on the phone said. I froze, holding my breath as I listened hard, hearing but not wanting to believe…that voice, was it really Budu?

"Kim?" the husky voice continued at the other end of the line.

"Hi," I managed to say. I had to clear my throat several times as the sounds would barely come out.

"How have you been? How are you holding up? Is Bugz taking care of you?" I swallowed the lump in my throat before answering. "I am fine. Bugz has offered to take care of me, but I declined."

"So how are you getting money?" he said. I shook my head in dismay as memories of the flashy, fast life invaded my thoughts.

"I have a job. I am working as a cashier and I am going back to school."

He laughed. "School, you and I know that shit aint for you," he said but I remained silent.

"I didn't know you had interest in going back to school, work and all that shit. You made it clear to me that you want to be kept," he continued.

"Well shit happened and things changed so," I said tersely.

"Mmmmmmmmm," was all he said. I tried to loosen up and sound a bit more concerned.

"How are you? How are you holding up? How are they treating you in there?" I asked him.

"I can't get into that. My allotted phone time is about to end but I just wanted to let you know that I still love you and I miss you. You haven't visited me since the ordeal but it's all good. That's what's up. All the best with your new life", then the call ended; I had no time to respond.

I really wanted to visit him after the arrest but was afraid. I missed him terribly but I suppressed that feeling. But now, hearing his voice made the feelings and thoughts resurface. I cried uncontrollably and secretly hoped he was coping in prison. That phone call disturbed the great studying mojo I had going previously. Now all I wanted to do was lie in bed, relax and clear my mind.

****

That night when Bugz showed up at the house, I met him outside instead of inviting him inside, because I desperately wanted to avoid mother's inquisition. We talked for hours. He, too, was proud of my new interest in school. Budu had directed him to cut off any form of assistance, financial or otherwise on the grounds that I had bailed on him and now had other men in my life. Budu knew I loved life in the fast lane and his call had been just a ploy to find out how I was really doing now that he was not there to bankroll me. Not just that, he also knew how much I loved to fuck. I can't think of any sane woman who is willing to wait for a man to do so many years in prison and not move on with another man. It was unfortunate how things had unfolded, I told Bugz, but I had to get on with my life. Declaring that he still had my best interest at heart, Bugz insisted that I shouldn't hesitate to ask him for help with anything, despite what Budu had said.

By the time I went back inside it was almost midnight. My cell phone showed 10 missed calls from Jemar. I called him back and without giving it much thought told him I had been busy studying and that my cell phone was on silent. Little did I know that lie would only add fuel to the fire. Jemar was talking to me so aggressively it's as if he would have hit me through the phone. I had never before heard him like that. I was lost for words when he blurted out, "are you fucking him?"

"Fucking who? What are you talking about?" I responded sounding a little confused. That's when I found out he had showed up to my house after calling me several times on my cell phone and there was no answer. So he apparently watched me the whole time conversing with Bugz and the fact that I hugged him and kissed him on the cheek before he left, only made things look worse for me. There was no placating Jemar tonight. As far as he was concerned, I had betrayed him and his fury was justified. I tried to explain that Bugz was just an old friend, but he didn't believe especially since I had lied to him about studying. Jemar hung up on me. I tried calling him back several times after but there was no response. This was our first argument, so I wasn't worried. I think he needed a few hours or a day to cool down before things could go back to the way they were. He just needed some time to himself. At least that's what I told myself, and really hoped I was correct.

SAY WHAT'S ON YOUR MIND

A few days passed; there was still no word from Jemar. He dealt with me more professionally than ever before on the job. I worked with it because I didn't want our nosy co-workers to sense that we were having issues. I really thought he was overreacting if this was still just about me talking to Bugz that night. He answered my calls but made no attempt to prolong the conversation. We didn't have lunch nor did anything together. He was really starting to irritate me. I asked for money to get my hair done, something he usually gave willingly; now, he shot me down. I knew something was definitely wrong. I wondered if he planned to fire me.

I sat my first Mathematics test and scored a B+, so I shared the good news with him. After all, he was the one funding my course yet he acted as if he didn't care. I couldn't take it anymore so I cornered him in his office.

"What have I done to you Jemar? You haven't paid me much attention of late, and I don't like it." He didn't even look at me and instead kept focussing on the heap of paper work before him.

"Jemar, can you look at me?"

"What Kimberly...What the hell do you want?"

I was appalled by his response. It was as if I was now a nuisance.

"What is bothering you?"

"You are bothering me Kim. You are my fucking problem. I thought I knew you. I really thought I knew you but I don't need to be around you anymore."

"Babe…I."

"Don't call me that."

"I don't understand where all this was coming from?"

"This is the result of me not taking the time to know you before I got involved. So now I found out that you were basically a whore not to mention the fact that you were with a drug king pin or maybe you are still with him. I don't know when someone will bust my door down and kill me. I am not about that kind of life and clearly that's all you knew."

I stood there and listened to him finally release his built up frustration.

"You can keep your job. After all you are temporary but after the cashier's maternity leave ends you are out of here. I don't want any form of personal relationship with you. So please come to work, do your job and leave me the hell alone."

I wanted to cuss him out and tell him he could keep his fucking cashier job but I needed it. Job hunting was so hard. I wasn't ready to go back there. I had at least two months to spare before I had to worry about employment again.

"Don't you ever call me a whore," I said as I slapped him across the face and stormed out of the office. I couldn't wait for this day to end.

FUCK IT ALL

Jemar thought I needed his pathetic ass. He thought I needed his chump change. I can make triple that amount in a day. He really thought he was doing me a favour. I am a bad bitch. I can have any man I want. This pussy of mine was so good. None of his other uptown bitches can fuck him like I did. He is going to be sorry he gave up this ass. "Fucking punk, fuck you Jemar," I screamed at the top of my lungs inside my house. Nosy neighbours walking by stared inside, further igniting my wrath. "What…fuck you too?" I screamed at them. I didn't need to go to school. Why the fuck was I doing that? I screamed and smashed a glass against the wall. I felt so angry. I needed a spliff; I needed drugs, something to calm me down and I knew just the person who could help me. I headed to Bugz's house.

****

Arriving just in time for the fresh stash of cocaine nicely laid on the counter, I grabbed a straw and sniffed a long line. "Hey, easy there, save some for later," I heard Bugz say. "Shit, I needed that." I said rubbing my nose.

"Rough day huh? That job thing is frustrating you now?" I didn't respond to Bugz. Instead I sniffed another half line. "That's it. That's how you do it baby," Anastasia whispered in my ear. I suddenly felt excited; excited and horny. That coke had to be laced with some other shit. I stood up and danced to the music playing in my head. I wanted to jump, scream and do some back flips, anything to show how damn good I was feeling. I moved my legs, swayed my hips, flung my head back and danced to deafening imaginary music. I felt like someone was controlling my movements until I felt a dick rubbing across my ass. I looked down at Anastasia who remained carefree on the couch. She smiled and winked at me as my pussy thumped. Though my judgment was clouded by the drugs, her smile didn't seem very approving but for some strange reason I bent to kiss her nevertheless. She invited me into her mouth with no resistance. I became even more excited and my inner thighs became damp with my own vaginal secretions. Our tongues flicked vigorously in unison and I dripped even more. The drugs were completely in control now. Anastasia grabbed my breasts and squeezed them. Bugz lifted my skirt and grabbed my ass while using the other hand to stroke my clit. They were caressing my entire body, and I didn't know what to do with myself. I was defenceless. Lying naked on the couch gazing up at the ceiling, I felt really good; I felt free from all worries. This felt so good. Damn, who needs people when you have drugs?

Next thing I knew I was in the doggy position and a dick was inside me. I couldn't tell if Bugz had a condom on or not, I was that fucked up. What I do remember is him shoving several fingers up my ass while pounding my pussy. Thank goodness our fucking spree didn't last more than one minute. After about three strokes his dick erupted like a fucking volcano. He hissed his teeth and slumped down in the couch. I guess he was pissed about coming so fast. I didn't pay him much attention. I had accepted that some men were mere one minute men, SIMPLY PUT. After our escapade, I sniffed a half line of cocaine one last time and watched as Bugz and Anastasia walked out the room and before I even realized it, I was out like a light.

LIFE AS I KNOW IT

The next few weeks were whatever. I lived young, wild and free. YOLO was my motto. I was back to my old self. I was making money, meeting and fucking well established men, I had my share of cocaine, I was in part- time dealings with Bugz, I had my expensive shit once more, I had the latest gadgets, designer bags, clothes, shoes plus I still had that little job at the pharmacy. The bitches at work were wondering who I was dating because I had everything going well. I was happy. As for school, I went to classes now and then but it was neither here nor there. I studied and did assignments when I felt like. I really didn't care about anything other than money. After all, having Maths and English would not have allowed me to make money quickly anyway. The academic route took time, and I couldn't be bothered.

Jemar became all concerned about how I had changed but whenever he tried to lecture me, I would always shut him up by saying I was doing what I know best, which is being a whore. Then I would throw in the "isn't that what you said to me or isn't that what you called me?" line. He claimed I was disrespectful and even threatened to fire me, and I told him to go right ahead. I didn't care. I had got my shit together and that's all that mattered.

I also started to visit Budu regularly – at least twice per week and brought him food sometimes. He questioned my sudden change of heart, but I never gave a straight answer. Instead, I would lighten the mood by telling him I am a bad bitch and was merely handling my business. He was my business and would always be. This line got him all the time. Even though Budu would be behind bars for a long time, I still felt connected to him.

As for Bri, she was the closest thing to a friend I had. I couldn't make her knowledgeable of all my dirty ways, but made it clear that I loved men, money and sex. She didn't need to know the details of how I went about handling my business. I didn't want her to judge me or spoil the little bond we had. I enjoyed our telephone conversations, I enjoyed partying with her; I enjoyed just about everything about her.

This was what I knew. This was the life I chose. This was life as I knew it.

THE RESORT

By: Temptress

The moment I had been eagerly anticipating all week finally arrived. What seemed to be the longest eight-hour work shift finally ended, and I hurried home to prepare for my first romantic get away with Alex. He had always suggested taking me out of town for a weekend, and I always refused but not this time. After all, I was a little stressed from work and needed a break-a good break too.

I tried to pack all the things I thought I would have possibly needed. As I did, my mind fast- forwarded to how the weekend would likely unfold. The more I thought about it, the more anxious I became. I watched the clock, eagerly awaiting his red Range Rover to pull up in my driveway. When he finally did, I felt a knot in my stomach. "Here we go" I said to myself as I closed the door.

He greeted me with a smile as I entered the vehicle but then proceeded to his telephone conversations. From one telephone call to another, his usual routine, but I didn't mind this time because this gave me time to settle my jitters and compose myself. I must say he looked very sexy in his white linen shirt, collar and cuffs undone, with his exquisitely sculptured mouth I was yearning to kiss. I let my hair down and let my mind wander as I basked in the cool country breeze.

The glamorous all inclusive resort seduced me with its sweeping water views, a private island and its white sandy beach. The hotel lobby had a chic contemporary décor with vivid murals and ceramics, intricate pearlescent tile work and graphic black and white photography. Fresh splashes of aqua blue fabric and lime green furniture offset the striking white architecture. The ambience was perfect. We checked in quickly and made our way to the suite. It was very welcoming. I loved the swan and heart shapes that were created using towels neatly placed in the centre of the king sized bed. The room also boasted a private ocean breeze balcony that had an amazing view of the poolside. Alex popped the bottle of champagne, then we drank to "happiness and new beginnings".

It was then time to try on all the things he bought for me on his trip. I always looked forward to the products of his shopping sprees because he had exquisite taste in women's clothing; a quality you rarely found in males. The things he purchased always had a way to highlight my figure. However, what was interesting about this shopping spree was a little black dress with the sides and the back cut out. The style of this dress didn't facilitate the use of a bra or underwear. It was interesting because I had recently purchased a dress similar and he had described it as distasteful and revealing, insisting that it would make me look trashy. Not sure if it was the alcohol clouding his judgment or the fact that he bought it, because here he was marvelling at how gorgeous I looked in the dress. Since he loved it so much, I decided to wear it to dinner.

After all the fitting excitement was over, we went to shower. The sight of his naked body immediately aroused me. With one arm around his waist, I pressed my jutting nipples to his back and with my other hand began to massage his cock. Slowly at first, and then with all the vigour I could muster. The water streamed down our naked bodies and every nerve came alive. He groaned and a wild wantonness beset me. He turned to face me and I knelt before him. I looked at him, fully erected and pulsating with anticipation and began to stroke him again. I had never sucked a dick before but was about to do it like a professional in this shower. Every man loves having his cock sucked, so it's a skill I believe every woman should learn. Still stroking him, I then kissed the tip of his cock. His groan sent shivers through me, so I opened my mouth to receive his fully erect cock. He tasted nice and fresh. I grasped his buttocks and began pulling on him, enjoying the feast. I began a rhythm of sucking him from base to head, stopping there momentarily to trace circles around the head of his desire with my tongue.

I reached to finger his full, tight balls as I continued to dive down on his cock, kneading and massaging simultaneously with the rhythm of my tongue. Head held back, eyes rolled over, his soft groans urged me to move faster and pull him as far as possible into my throat. My head moved up and down as I thrived on the excitement of him growing even harder as I devoured him.

Alex and I had not had sex throughout the period we were together, and there was never any mention of it. The closest he had ever gotten to seeing me naked was the time he showed up at my house unexpectedly. Now there was some mutual unspoken language between us. "Uggh !" He pushed me back then leaned forward and kissed me. Exiting the shower he told me not to move. I wanted him so badly, right then and there in the shower.

Seconds later he lunged at me with a condom on his cock, pushing me against the shower wall. Before I knew it, he had both my hands in one of his in a vice-like grip above my head as he pinned me to the wall. "Oh fuck" I moaned as I eagerly anticipated his well erected nine inch cock inside my wet, throbbing pussy. He grabbed my hair and thrust inside me, pulled out and thrusting again with even more vengeance. It was slightly painful but I loved it. His other arm pulled my hair, bringing my face up and his lips were now on mine. I moaned into his mouth giving his tongue an opening. His tongue expertly explored my mouth. He was the only person who could get me wet with just one kiss. He kissed me in such a way that words could not describe. My tongue tentatively stroked his in a slow erotic dance that was all about touch and sensation, all bump and grind. He bent me over once again, gripped my waist and held me in place. He fucked me even harder, slapping my ass simultaneously. My moans were now constant and high pitched as I somehow searched for an area to grip on the slippery walls of the shower. He then pulled out and led me to the Jacuzzi where I plopped down on his cock and rode it like a jockey. I watched myself in the mirror and marvelled at the sight of me expertly straddling that cock like a porn star. I whined, twisted, bounced and did everything I possibly could. He then stood up and thrust into me a few more times then pulled out. He held my face, looked at me then kissed me. "You will get more later," he said, leaving me in the middle of the bathroom even hornier than before. My legs were wobbly, and my mind was swirling at the memory of what had just happened.

My pussy was dripping even more as I sat on the Jacuzzi and watched him shower, attempting to regain my composure. He turned to face me "aren't you coming to wash off, it's almost time for us to leave for dinner." I just smiled. I was still basking in the moment but managed to get up and join him. I desperately wanted to skip dinner.

EIGHT RIVERS RESTAURANT

I slipped into the little sheer black dress with strategically placed panels to protect my modesty and at which Alex had marvelled earlier; however, now he insisted I wear shorts instead, claiming he was in an ass mood. Alex was a handful, but I granted his request and changed outfit. He was looking like a debonair gentleman in his fitted denim jeans, cardigan and loafers. I felt proud in his presence.

Alex placed his hands firmly in the small of my back holding me in a commanding way. It was a gesture that said "you are mine". We had heads turning the moment we left the suite. I could feel the stares piercing my skin and a renewed confidence, as I did everything a bit more than the norm. The way I walked and swayed my hips was more pronounced than ever before. I was motivated by the stares, and I didn't hesitate to show off.

Unfortunately, upon arrival at the restaurant, the maitre d advised that we would not be allowed to enter dressed as I was in shorts.

"What?" Alex exclaimed, "I called the front desk and I was told that females were allowed to wear shorts but not jeans." The man stood his ground.

"I am sorry sir, but I cannot allow you inside with the female dressed like that."

"I told you I should have worn the dress," I whispered, clinging to his arms.

"Just great, now I have to head back to the suite, passing the very people I was just showing off on."

Alex laughed. "I am sure those people were busy minding their own business. Besides who cares if they notice the changes. At least you look hot." We both laughed.

I was not enjoying the walk to our room even though the distance was short. It was the fact that I had to climb so many flights of stairs because our room was located at the newly established section of the hotel which surprisingly had no elevators in operation. The renovation process was still underway.

I stopped in the hallway for a few minutes and took a few pictures before heading inside to change.

Several minutes later, I gladly slipped into the little sheer dress that gripped my enviable figure.

Alex looked at me and smiled uncontrollably. "Do you like what you see?"

"I love it," he said with arms outstretched as he cautiously led me through the door. We took a different route this time, where a new set of eyes complimented my new attire. The host smiled as we made our entry. "See that wasn't so bad. Please give me a minute to prepare your table."

"Thank you," Alex and I said in unison.

"Turn slightly and show off the sexy slits at the side of your dress," Alex said.

"What?" I looked at him puzzled. "Go ahead, flaunt your sexiness, the guy at the table is staring at you." I laughed.

Alex continued to amaze me.

As we walked to our table, his remarks occasionally made me slightly uncomfortable. I was not sure I liked the idea of him bragging about me or maybe it was slightly awkward because I was not used to him relating to me that way. After all, it was the first time we were really going to spend quality time together. I still had not uttered the words, officially making him my man but he made me feel like his woman. It became even worse the moment we were introduced to our server for the night.

"Isn't she gorgeous?" he asked. "Yes she is. You are a very lucky man." I could have slapped the waiter for encouraging the idle talk, but then the man was only doing his job. I supposed flattery may have granted him a few extra tips.

"She makes me happy," Alex further stated. All this attention made me edgy.

"Do you want to see a picture of the outfit she had on earlier? She was too sexy, we had to go back and change?" he prolonged the conversation with the waiter. If the look I gave Alex had the power of death, he would have gone to meet his maker in that instant. Why on earth would he even suggest showing the waiter, a complete stranger, pictures of me? I was uncomfortable; but he, on the other hand, seemed so playful, so happy and relaxed in showing me off to strangers. I desperately hoped the waiter would do his damn job and bring the menus or go serve a table instead of this socializing. I breathed a sigh of relief when he offered to bring us wine. That was the best thing he had said all night. I watched as he filled our glasses and hoped he would not say anything else to Alex. Fortunately for me, he stuck to the script – served the wine, provided the menus and left. He must have read my mind.

Alex gave me a brief lecture on dining etiquette. I was accustomed to just one knife and a fork whenever I set the table at home. So I was glad when he began explaining the difference between the salad/dessert and main course silverware. The take home point was to "begin at the outside and work in" towards the plate.

"I know you are accustomed to people holding the wine glass like a cup but you are to actually hold it by the stem," he said, picking up his glass and demonstrating. Fearful of using the wrong silverware, I made sure to follow his lead.

I was enjoying the meal, the ambience and Alex's company. Everything was perfect, when the mood was interrupted by a phone call. The receptionist who was his good friend was apparently calling to find out how things were going, having made the reservations for the suite and restaurant. For a brief moment my insecurities resurfaced and I wondered if she was someone he had fucked. I didn't put anything past him but opted to dismiss the thought and focussed instead on us.

The friendly chatter with the waiter continued for the rest of the night, but I tolerated it as best as I could. I enjoyed the divine gourmet dining that featured continental cuisine with a distinctly Caribbean flair. By the time we got to dessert, I was satiated. Alex attempted to feed me ice cream on several occasions but I just could not consume anything else. So I lay in the warmth of his arms and allowed him to finish his dessert. We cuddled, conversed and enjoyed what was left of a beautiful evening.

A LIL VIBE

After consuming all that food, sleep was the next pressing issue for me. I glanced at Alex who seemed so energized even as I was struggling to stay awake. He clearly wasn't ready to go back to the room, so we walked the hotel grounds and sampled some of the entertainment. First, we endured a young man playing a piano and chanting the lyrics of songs that sounded like they were recorded in the 13th century. I sat quietly and rocked and was more entertained by Alex enjoying the ensemble. He ordered another drink. How was he still drinking? I felt so mellow from the mimosa, vodka, chardonnay and rum cream even one more drink would have been too much.

He told me to loosen up and drink to my heart's content. I relaxed, secure in the knowledge that I was in good hands. Unfamiliar with the songs, I began to lose interest and was falling asleep when the pianist suddenly changed tempo with a Sam Cooke selection which caught my attention. "That's *the sound of the men working on the chain gaaanng. All day long they are saying HUUUH, AAHHH"* I was finally able to sing along. After a few more hits, the vibe and the spectators dwindled, so Alex and I left. We then watched the entertainment coordinators teaching people how to do a few of the more popular dance moves in dancehall. This was hilarious especially when the DJ played Mr Vegas' 'Bruck it dung'. Most of the women were completely out of sync with the rhythm. Alex beckoned for me to go join them but I was much too tired. I was already struggling to keep my eyes open much less dance.

"Get up there. Show them how it's done."

"No babe…I prefer to watch."

"Please, do it for me, I have never seen you dance. Remember this weekend is all about fun. Just let loose and enjoy yourself."

"No… I am tired," I said.

"Are you serious? Here I was hoping that we could go clubbing after?" Alex said sounding a little disappointed.

"Yes we can but just allow me to take a power nap; 20 minutes, no disturbance is all I need" I reassured him. So we headed back to the room. "Are you sure you won't feel tired waiting in the room while I sleep?"

"I think I will go back downstairs to watch the entertainment and return at 12 to wake you." He planted warm kisses along my neck and lips before leaving.

It wasn't long before I dozed off. I awoke to the sound of Alex struggling to open the door.

"Time to get up," he said kissing my cheeks."

"Thank you, I feel so much better."

"Are you sure you have the energy to party?" I asked.

"Yes I am fine, now let's go." I rushed to the bathroom, brushed my teeth, refreshed my makeup and headed for the club.

****

I felt over dressed in mini dress and heels compared to the other women dressed in jeans pants or shorts with ordinary tops and flip flops. No accessories, no outrageous hair styles, no heels, no nothing. They were simply attired. To top off my feeling of being too over dressed, the DJ's were not playing to my liking either. They played out each song and "pulled it up" so many times, it was beginning to annoy me. Still, I was determined Alex and I were going to have a good time.

"Just be yourself babe, don't feel shy around me," he urged. He laughed. He had no idea who he was dealing with, so I just sat in his lap, rocked and whined slowly, occasionally, just to make him stop fussing about me not having a good time. It wasn't long before the DJ finally began playing my jams. I wasn't wearing any panties so I seductively bend over in front of Alex, gyrated to the floor then back up, bracing against him ensuring that my ass was pressing against his cock. I jiggled my ass, as I continued to brace against him. I could feel the hardness nudging between the crack of my ass. He spun me around, pulled me closer, nudged between my legs then suddenly inserted two fingers inside my warmth unexpectedly. I squirmed and pulled myself away. He smiled rudely at me. "Your pussy is so wet."

I kind of liked it when he spoke dirty. This sent shivers down my spine and even more secretions from my vagina. Alex had the power to make me drip on the spot with just one touch. I could see it in his eyes that he wanted to fuck me now but I would tease him a bit more first. It gave me pleasure to see the want in his eyes, and

I could feel it in his every move. I was definitely enjoying this moment. I urged him to sit on one of the stools then threw my hands around his neck and wrapped one of my legs around his waist, now giving him full view of my moist, bare pussy, then I pulled myself closer and rubbed it along his crotch. The feel of his hard cock on my bare clit almost made me come on the spot. We were suddenly interrupted by the DJ who had several announcements to make.

Alex used the opportunity to leave. He gave me the keys and told me to drive. When we got to the hotel, I lay on the bed waiting for him to undress. I watched every crevice of his body; the well chiselled chest, small gold cross around his neck, his juicy ass and long curved cock. He expertly slipped on a condom, draped my body with his hands then kissed my neck, and I felt the hardness nudging between the crack of my ass once again. I turned to face him. "You are so beautiful," he murmured while cupping my breasts. Alex knew what he was doing. His years of experience were working as he touched my body in ways that seemed as if he was trying to wipe the memory of every other man I had ever been with, to stamp my skin with the permanence of his own stroke. I felt the heat of envy: what other women is he messing with, who is giving him this confidence, this command? I turned again and Alex slipped in from behind, and before I knew it, the orgasms were tripping over each other and seizing me up. I clutched his fingers and he clutched mine. My whole body arched and the aftershock lingered for a while. We lay in each other's arms and drifted off to sleep.

SURREAL WEEKEND

Alex was still sleeping soundly. I would definitely have to get used to sleeping with someone who snored. I often times wondered if I snored, but I can't recall ever being told that. I grabbed the fruit plate and snack, slid the glass doors open and sat on the balcony basking in the view. I inhaled the scent of fresh, crisp air and watched the palm trees swaying in the wind. I watched as the staff prepared the bar/dining area for the stampede of hungry people that would soon fill it up. I gazed at the ripples from the mini water fall that cascaded into the pool. I looked at my phone. I had not been paying much attention to it. I had about one hundred messages from various social networks to regular text messages. I scrolled through in an attempt to respond to a few persons when Alex snuck behind me on the balcony, snatched the phone then rushed back to the room.

"Let me take care of that for you," he said with a huge grin on his face.

"Please give it back"

"Not on your life, sweetheart, you are mine for the weekend." He then turned the phone off, walked over to the closet, entered a code to open the safe, and ensured that my view was hindered. He then placed the phone inside and promptly closed it. He spun around to see the look of absolute shock on my face.

"What the hell do you think you are doing? I need my phone Alex. Anything could happen."

"What am I doing?" he countered. "I'm being selfish. I know you are always available to your family and friends, but this weekend, I have no intentions of sharing you with anyone else. That means no interruptions."

I stared at him dumfounded.

"Fine" I said, folding my arms. You put your phone in as well."

"I am a business person sweetie, I can't do that." I scuffed, grabbed my robe and headed towards the shower. Typical of him, I thought. I know fully well that he will be busy texting Lord knows who. UGH MEN! I refused to argue with him over a phone. I just wanted to enjoy my last day at the resort before going back to the daily routine of being overworked and underpaid. Alex and I showered quickly then headed to the dining area for breakfast.

I had three hash browns, a Spanish omelet, croissant, French toast, three strips of bacon, scrambled eggs, callaloo, tomato smothered in a melted cheese sauce with a glass of apple juice and a fruit plate. Alex looked at me as if I was greedy, but I didn't care. He on the other hand stuck to the conventional breakfast of fried dumplings with ackee and salt fish with a glass of orange juice. Being filled was an understatement. I definitely had to give thanks for such a wonderful breakfast. About half hour later we were off to the pool side.

Alex insisted on watching me swim rather than join me. Of course I couldn't help but get an attitude when I saw him on his phone. So unfair, I thought once again. I am supposed to believe that he is "doing business", UGH. I looked away and made conversation with the other ladies in the pool. One hour had passed and his ass was still not in the pool.

"Do you plan to join me anytime soon?" I asked with a slight attitude.

"Yes I will but I prefer to go by the nude beach," he said.

I was not that confident with my body and sexuality. I knew I would have been uncomfortable, even though that was the general attire for everyone there, but I stupidly agreed to it. This weekend was about me stepping out of my comfort zone. We gathered our belongings and waited patiently for the boat that transported the guests to the secluded island. I really did not want to do this but I was YOLOing my way through all the new experiences, and therefore was willing to try anything once.

As the boat approached the island, my eyes were fixed on those who had arrived prior to us. The minute you stepped off the boat, your clothes were to come off – those were the rules. I stood motionless. I wanted to get back on that boat and head back to the resort; back to civilization with people sporting their bikinis, getting tanned, relaxing on lawn chairs, sipping smoothies or reading a novel. I didn't want to be here on an island with naked people, and I certainly didn't want to be one of them. My eyes ached from seeing so many variations of body parts all coming at me. There were saggy breasts, acne-filled ass, bushy vaginas, light skinned people with dangerously black private parts– and this was not even the tip of the iceberg of how unpleasant the scenery was. I wished the ground would open, swallow me and spit me out on the beach back at the resort. Alex undressed and waited patiently for me to do the same, which took me about half hour if not longer. The boat had even made several trips to and from the island before I finally managed to undress. If Alex wasn't so vigilant, I would have made a run for it. I watched him as he walked comfortably. Why am I even surprised that he loved this. He seemed to always be intrigued by anything with any form of sexual connotation. I wondered how many women he had taken here. I desperately yearned for this to be over.

I must have had the most awkward walk on the beach; I tried desperately to cover my breasts with my hands and my vagina with my inner thighs as I walked. The IMPOSSIBLE, if you ask me but I had to try something. I was losing my mind. I guess Alex sensed my discomfort, so he placed his arms around my waist in an attempt to soothe my jitters, but my eyes traversed the island frantically in my quest to locate a secluded spot on the beach. My paranoia was at its peak. "Babe relax," Alex said then lifted me over his shoulder. Oh my God, the whole beach is probably staring up my ass now," I thought as embarrassment swallowed me up. He then let me down beside one of the palm trees. I looked around and wondered how big the island was. We seemed to be away from the others. It was a nice little spot Alex had found. I felt better now that I was surrounded by trees.

Dropping the bag to the ground, he immediately cupped my face with his hands devouring my mouth with such ferocity I was forced up against the tree. His body anchored me in position as he pulled a condom out of the bag and slide it on in record time. This is so wild but interesting, I thought. I had been terrified to walk along the beach nude, yet here I was about to fuck. He hoisted my legs up to wrap around his waist and I curled my arms tight around his neck with my back against the enormous trunk of the tree. It was rough, and I felt something poke me occasionally but ignored it and hoped it wouldn't bruise my skin. I was completely hot and horny that I don't think I really cared if it did. He slammed into me, and it was glorious. He did it again and again, and it was even more glorious as he impaled me again and again and I enjoyed it. I stared up at the sky and released my howl in honour of its magnificence. He exploded inside me as our carnal desire for each other was finally given physical recognition. For a brief moment I wondered if anyone heard or saw us.

We laid on the sand for hours with our bodies pressed against each other, talking about absolutely nothing in particular, playing, laughing and teasing each other. It's as if we were in a world of our own. It was soon time for us to check out so we headed back to the entrance, got dressed and signalled the boat to come get us. The joy I felt when the clothes returned to my body. While the sex was mind- blowing, I was never going to another nude beach.

Upon returning to the resort, we hurried to the room, packed our bags, showered, got dressed and I took one last, long deep breath as I closed the door behind us. My surreal weekend was coming to an end. We loaded the bags into the car then returned for lunch which was just as sumptuous as breakfast. We lingered around the resort for a short while, took several photos then headed home.

THE REAL QUESTION.....LOVE OR DICK WHIPPED?

Still on a high from our getaway, I asked Alex to accompany me to a cocktail party/dinner endorsed by the nursing association that day. Unfortunately, he was unable to attend and could not pick me up afterwards. The only compromise was for him to take me there. Forty-five minutes before we were slated to leave, Alex had the nerve to send a text asking to confirm the time of the event. I grabbed my cell phone and dialled him immediately.

"What do you mean by what time is the event? I have been reminding you about this all day then you are going to be asking me this at a time when you should be on your way?"

"I am sorry. I got so caught up with some stuff that I forgot about your event. I am so tired I don't think I can travel that distance to you. Can you meet me half way?"

"No I will call a cab. Don't worry about it." I said. Truth be told, anger was ripping through my flesh. How could you ask me to meet you half way on public transportation when I was all dolled up in my sexy dress and six inch heels, FORTY FIVE minutes prior to the time the event began? Still I played it cool and caught a cab.

The dinner turned out ok even though I was terribly late. I didn't feel like spilling the details to Alex at the end of it all so instead, I tweeted "Should have gotten drunk, but it was a great night" before retiring to bed.

Alex was not the type of person to let something go without somehow blaming you for something even when he was wrong. Over time, I came to realize a few things about him. It was his style to make reference to things he had done for you in the past whenever we argued then gave the impression that you were this ungrateful person. This worked on my nerves all the time. He had to have the last say at all times; so the next day the drama began. The first of a barrage of text messages read:

"Briana, I hate feeling like I am not appreciated. I like you and I make tremendous effort to do things for you despite being busy. At times I may not be able to do things but I certainly don't make unreasonable proposals. I make promises intending to fulfil them but if I don't at times, I don't expect to be hit over the head with a hammer. I simply couldn't travel that distance to your home to take you to the dinner, especially since it was during peak hour so I would encounter a lot of traffic and I was already so exhausted from the day's events which is why I asked you to meet me half way. I would have taken you. A little understanding would have been better but no instead you pissed me off and went all over the place with someone else which shows you don't really care. I hope you got drunk as you wished and enjoyed whatever you did after. As you said it was a great night. For what it's worth my night was bad. But as you said, I don't need to focus my energy on you. Thanks for that comment. You are feisty enough to respond without thinking. But what's new?"

I read his message in disbelief. I didn't understand what this man was talking about. "Got drunk and enjoyed whatever with whomever." What the fuck? He could be so paranoid and jealous; it was so pathetic. The moment there was a disagreement he immediately assumed you had either found another man or were interested in someone else. It was my theory that people who were guilty of something were often the ones to constantly accuse others of those very actions. I ignored the message but then it dawned on me that I tweeted something about having a great night. Was he stalking my twitter account and personalizing my post? Was this what it boiled down to now, checking social networks and arguing with me re a post? If I was right, and he was going to judge me based on something I posted, then we were in for a whole lot of drama because my posts were not for the weak. A few minutes later, another message came in.

"You really lack humility. You don't know when you are wrong. You don't know how to say sorry and you know why that is Briana?? Because you think you don't need anyone. Look around and think back on what people have done for you in your life and tell me if you really don't need anyone."

At this point I was beyond confused. All I said was that I would call a cab and all of a sudden I was acting like I didn't need anyone? Furthermore, what on earth was I supposed to apologize for? I was not in the mood for this unnecessary drama.

"So with all that said, what do you propose that I do?" I responded.

"That's what you have to say Briana, have you really read what I wrote?"

Then the impact of his message about me getting drunk and doing whatever with whomever really hit home. Nothing pissed me off more than when a man accused me wrongfully. I became even angrier.

"I have had it with you. Let me be with 'my lack of humility and ungratefulness' you are so quick to highlight. Leave me alone Alex".

He must have called about 50 times afterwards, but I ignored all his calls.

"Can you answer your phone or respond to my text messages and extend some courtesy to me?" Two minutes later, "Briana, answer your phone please? You are so stubborn." Seconds later another text came in, "God damn it Briana, answer your phone so we can have a civilized conversation."

Ten minutes later, "Baby you can come and see me today. You know what they say; there is nothing like make up sex."

I still did not respond. Two hours later, I received another text message, "I will come get you at 6 tonight."

"Its peak hour so the traffic will be hectic. Wouldn't want you driving all this way for such an ungrateful person," I typed with sarcasm. There was no response. Several hours passed before another message. "I am so down right now and I could really use your company. I don't like it when we fuss, it affects me too much. I become so miserable."

I hated when we argued as well, especially over petty issues. I wanted to see him but was still angry.

"Can you please let me come for you?" he asked once more.

"Fine," I responded.

When he arrived, I was actually happy to see him but made sure to contain my emotions. The moment I entered the car he held my hands and thanked me for coming. He held my hand for the remainder of the journey home, kissing my knuckles/my palms/fingers and cheeks periodically. I maintained a straight face regardless.

When we arrived at the house, we watched a movie and indulged in a glass of red wine. However, snuggling in his arms had an impact on me as usual. How does he do this to me? My heart raced and blood was pumping through my body, even my nipples could not ignore his presence. I felt the bulge rising from inside his pants as he kissed my neck. I teased and played a little before removing them. My palms longingly stroked the flesh of his cock, my fingers desperate to knead his balls. He groaned in unison with my touch. I got on my knees and gently darted my tongue back and forth on the tip, eliciting a slick of salty juice that casually cascaded over his rim. I gripped his firm, muscled buttocks as I continued to nibble and suck his cock, taking a little more of him in my mouth, stroke by stroke. My mouth was all encompassing and his long black cock teased the back of my throat. I loved doing this and couldn't deny the burning flame it ignited between my thighs as I continued to suck even deeper and stronger. I then pulled all the way to the back of my throat, wrapping my lips around his base. I felt the throbbing and knew he was about to explode. I pulled away and his liquid spilled on my breast as he convulsed at his climax. I stayed on my knees and watched him come back to reality.

"Why don't you let me come in your mouth? I would love if you swallowed." I was not about swallowing anything but food and my saliva.

"Have you ever tried it?" he asked.

"No and I am not planning to, it's just not something I do," I said firmly.

"Ok sweetheart," he said, slipping on the rubber.

He lifted me off my knees, gently placed me on the bed then slowly and deeply plunged into my vagina. He maintained this slow tempo but with each thrust penetrated deeper. At one point I felt his cock poke me in my belly. I pierced my fingers into his back as he plunged deeper inside of me. Even as I treasured this moment, I was afraid to let go and give my all because I had my doubts. My gut told me I was not the only one. There was no way a man like him could be committed to one person. Although my gut was usually on point, I had no intentions of going to search for trouble. A whirl of emotions flooded my body, and I broke out in tears. "Am I hurting you baby?" "No...No don't stop."

"Why are you crying then?" He eased off me, looking into my eyes. "You love me don't you?" My lips remained sealed. "Why won't you say it?" Trying to divert from the subject, I let my body respond. He held me closer and tighter than before as he thrust a few more times into my vagina, sending me into the orgasm my body so frantically, so desperately, so completely desired. A primal scream escaped.... "I think you love me" I heard him whisper softly in my ear, falling asleep shortly after with his head huddled between my breasts.

The real questions... Did I love him or was it the sex?

Can good sex bloom into true love?

DRAMA, DRAMA.......MORE DRAMA

These past weeks have been ridiculously busy. My days and nights seemed endless. I studied for final exams every chance I got. Even during the fifteen minute breaks I got at work. This was the moment I had been waiting for. I was only a few months away from becoming a registered nurse. I imagined that several things would change after I received my degree. The thought of me obtaining my Bachelor of Science in Nursing, already made me feel established and recognized. This would be my first big accomplishment. I was simultaneously nervous and excited. I feared failing, so I read just about every piece of literature I could. I paid more attention to just about everything at work, in the event that these practical situations could somehow help me in exams.

My social life added even more stress. Don't know if it was Karma or just a mere coincidence that I had been meeting or finding out about Alex's ex-girlfriends all in the same week. I tried not to make any assumptions or dig up unnecessary dirt about his past. I really did not want to know the details. But the more I ignored the stories, the girls, the pictures, the more things presented themselves. A mixture of anger and jealousy flooded my mind whenever I reflected on the barrage of women he had been with. He definitely had a history. There was no way he could just end a relationship and start a new one. I know somehow, somewhere along the line two or more women were being juggled. The thought of being cheated on once more lingered in my thoughts. A pain radiated through my stomach as I thought about how long he probably had been cheating on me and most importantly with whom? How did one end up in the same situation twice? Different person but yet the same outcome; I didn't get it. Was I destined to be cheated on? What was I not doing right? I felt my chest tighten as many more questions bombarded my mind.

Get it together Briana....get it together I told myself, as I took several deep breaths. The truth is, I had no evidence that Alex had, in fact, been cheating on me but then again how was I suppose to have evidence when I wasn't searching. Was he cheating? I begged The Lord to show me signs that would indicate whether or not Alex was cheating. I felt a bit of frustration. I pinched myself then took a deep breath, grabbed my anatomy textbook and allowed science to take control. I read and buried all my insecurities.

The last thing I remembered headlining the page was 'Functions of the Urinary System'. I am uncertain as to how long I had been sleeping but that rest was everything I needed and then some. A few minutes later Alex called asking me to accompany him out of town to a conference. Alex's conferences meant hotels, different scenery and tranquillity, so of course I agreed. Studying by the poolside with a long glass of mango strawberry smoothie, I smiled as I imagined the taste of the fruit splash. I gathered my study materials, packed my bag then warmed up my left over baked chicken with mashed potatoes, macaroni and cheese and watched a movie, while I waited for Alex.

****

When he eventually arrived, I could tell it was going to be a miserable journey to the country. The contortions in his face, knitted brows, the unintentional puckered lips and the way he glanced at things were always signs that he was miserable. I knew I should brace myself for the worst.

"You know I haven't prepared my presentation for tomorrow. I had so much to do today. Sometimes I wonder why I always have so much to do," he said releasing a long deep sigh.

"How about mentioning whatever comes to mind when you think about the topic and I will make jottings. That should get the ideas flowing then we try to put things together." He shrugged off my suggestion. I guess he was feeling very overwhelmed. I tried to make conversation with the idea to take his mind off the issue at hand but it didn't work. Instead, it seemed like everything I said irritated him, so I kept quiet for the rest of the journey, only responding to his questions.

By the time we got to the resort things got even worse. The room service was horrible, Wi-Fi was down which meant he could not work on the presentation he was already feeling overwhelmed about. Then to top it off, he left his shear, his undershirt and matching shoes to complement the outfit he had selected to wear to the presentation.

"I have a disposable razor that you could use" I said. However, he didn't acknowledge me; instead, he paced the room and hissed his teeth nonstop.

A text message came to my cell phone interrupting the silence. "Umm, can you put the phone on silent," he said tersely then headed towards the balcony.

The room phone rang; it was the operator calling for Alex. I called him, he answered but when I mentioned that there was someone on the phone to him, there was no answer. I figured he was really feeling overwhelmed and didn't want to talk to anyone so I took a message which was about the code for accessing the Wi-Fi. As I attempted to enter it on his laptop, Alex came in, looked around and got really upset. "What the hell do you think you are doing?"

"I am entering the password for the Wi-Fi," I said, glancing up at him briefly.

"Oh my God I don't believe you. You mean you have the password all this time Briana and kept it to yourself and you see the predicament I am in."

"No, I didn't have it. I just got it from the operator," I said trying to explain myself. He then grabbed the computer, hissed his teeth then said, "Briana don't upset me," as he headed back to the balcony. I don't fucking believe this man right now. I went outside to join him on the balcony, but he ignored me and stormed pass me a few seconds later as he headed back to the room. I couldn't hold back the tears. I knew he was under pressure but all I had been trying to do is help. I didn't understand why he was behaving like this. I placed the piece of paper with the Wi-Fi information on the table then went to the bathroom. He banged on the door. I opened it, still trying to wipe my tears.

"How did you even know how to get onto my computer?"

"It was already turned on"

Right then I knew this man had skeletons in his closet. Maybe he had a whole graveyard, if he was so upset that I apparently came in contact with his computer. I closed the door and spent the rest of the night in the bathroom. I no longer wished to stay in the same room with him.

I dropped to the restroom floor and cried. This door was the protective barrier from his anger. I texted Kim and had a brief conversation with her with the hope of cheering myself up. It wasn't long before she told me she was going to bed, so I was back to square one; alone with my sorrows. I then whispered a brief prayer.

I had never seen him this angry before and over what….something I considered petty.

"Lord, please get me through this night and this weekend." I think I must have dozed off for about an hour. The aggressive bangs on the door frightened me from my sleep. I listened as he begged me to come out and then when hours passed and I didn't, he cussed me about being stubborn, but I ignored it all. I came out on my own timing, snuggled under the sheets, hugged the pillows and cuddled myself to sleep.

The next morning, Alex hugged me and apologized for his behaviour. Now he felt like being nice, I thought. Now that his presentation was complete and everything was going as planned once again, I should return his affection as if nothing had happened. I didn't say anything. I watched him get dressed and listened to him talk. I couldn't wait for him to leave. My initial plans to study by the poolside would not make sense in my present state of mind. I needed to relax. I needed a break from him.

I picked up my razor and headed towards the bathroom to groom my bikini line.

"What are you doing?" he asked.

"I plan to go swimming, so I need to shave."

"I thought you were going to give me your razor," he said. I looked at him in amazement then handed it over. When I had suggested it last night he didn't even acknowledge me. I wasn't in the mood for another argument over something petty because I knew then that a major blow-up was in the making. The more time we spent together, the more I learnt about his really bad habits.

The minute he left the room I could feel the tension leaving my body. I quickly tried on my fringe swim top with shorts, took a few mirror pictures, applied my sunscreen then was off to the pool. This was exactly what I needed; TRANQUILITY.

I had a grand time alternating between the pool, hot tub, swim up bar, participating in water sports not to mention the water slide and the lazy river. The unlimited food and liquor definitely added to the grand time I was having. As I ate, I couldn't help eavesdropping on the conversation of a group of young ladies sitting across from me.

"Didn't he look hot in that suit this morning," one said.

"Yes he did. He is always well dressed. I think he is just naturally sexy..."

"I liked his presentation," her friend interjected.

"He seems like a decent man. I wonder if he has any kids or if he is married?" the first woman asked. At that point another friend joined the table and asked what they were discussing.

"The presenter this morning, I think his name is Alex."

"You know he is not as nice as he seems," said the woman who just joined the table. At this point they had my undivided attention. I paused chewing as I listened in on the rest of the woman's sentence.

"I heard he was with a pharmacist prior to this and beat her so badly that she had to leave him."

"Oh really, he doesn't look like that type."

A man who beats his woman doesn't always have a look," the latecomer shot back bitterly.

"Well we don't know if that is true; besides, people will always say bad things about you."

"Well in my opinion, if it nuh guh suh, it nearly guh suh." They all laughed.

Lord what is this? I thought. Was this a sign? Was this true? I sure as hell would not be sticking around to find out first hand if Alex was a woman -beater.

I didn't have an appetite anymore. I got up and headed back to the room. The woman's voice kept replaying in my thoughts. Did Alex really hit a woman? It was times like these that I wished God actually gave yes or no answers PRONTO. Did Alex really beat a woman or should I say beat his women? I asked myself once more. Why would someone even start a rumour like that? How were they benefitting from this? Was it a rumour? I had many unanswered questions.

I didn't know what to do. Even if this wasn't true there were still other factors that I needed to consider. Not to mention the mere coincidence of hearing stories of his past ALL week... Were these mere coincidences or a sign that I should remove myself from his life?

Alex didn't get back to the room until about ten that night. Of course he seemed back to his old self. "Go shower and give me that pussy. Tonight you are getting a no condom fuck." I held a straight face. I was not amused at all by this joke. That was not about to happen; not in this lifetime.

We showered and I laid tensely beside him. He then pulled me towards him and started licking my pussy. I was not in the mood and felt disgusted by the wet tongue sliding all over my clit. I held his head and stopped him. "You don't need to do this," I said but he continued. "Alex stop, I am not enjoying this." His tongue quit immediately. If there was ever a way to hurt him, it would be a direct hit to his ego, especially his sexual performance. He reached down and felt my vagina but I was dry as a bone. He was shocked by this because usually I would be dripping wet. "Wow, how is it that you're not wet?"

"I don't know," I responded.

"Let's not do this," he said. "Let's head home." Those words were music to my ears. I knew he was upset and had no choice but to patiently await his wrath. Nothing was in black and white with Alex. He HAD to analyze and conclude. Finally he would unleash, he just HAD to.

ANGER OR HIDDEN TRUTH?????

A very awkward pregnant silence prevailed on the journey home. I was very pensive, still analyzing the conversation I had overheard, but Alex kept interrupting my fragile thoughts with his incessant ramblings. "Who did you talk to when I left for the conference, because clearly something transpired while I was gone? Did you flirt with someone else and find some new interest? Is that why even during the foreplay you were not aroused? You are usually easily aroused but not this time. Is there something you need to say to me Briana?" A look of amazement flooded my face. Could someone be THAT insecure?

"Are you listening to yourself Alex? Have you really listened to the questions you just asked? Can you take a minute FOR ONCE and think logically about the situation? Do you think that maybe other factors may have contributed to my foul mood, for starters, the fact that you ignored me then cussed me out Friday night?"

"Didn't I apologize for that Briana?"

"So because you apologized means I should forget all that happened?"

Silence again. "Someone said that the last person you were with, you would beat her continuously and that's why she left you."

"Where the hell did you hear that? How is it that you are always hearing things? I have never laid hands on a woman. You are always listening to the crap that people say to you. Furthermore, why would they come to you of all persons and say that?"

"They didn't come to me. I overheard a conversation." I shot back immediately.

"You overheard a conversation?" he repeated. "And you expect me to believe this?"

"Believe whatever you want Alex," I said feistily.

"That is one of the things I dislike about you. You keep listening to "hearsay" and people's idle talk. Sometimes I wonder if you even have a mind of your own and I hate the fact that you keep protecting these people. Why you refuse to tell me who says these negative things is beyond me, then you claim you care about me. If you really cared you would tell me who is saying what."

"I really don't see the need to reveal the names," I said.

"You never see the need to tell me anything. You seem to pledge allegiance to people who are trying to tear me down. I dislike people because all they do is use me. I don't give a fuck about what anyone wants to say about me. I live for myself and God. I don't need to impress anyone else. I have had enough of you and your negative talk. I told you before I don't want to hear the bullshit being said about me yet you are still volunteering information."

I zoned out after that because this was his typical style. I am not sure he even gave a convincing answer as to whether or not he hit the woman. Then again, I don't think any man guilty of that would ever outright admit to it.

"Furthermore..." his voice drew me back, "If I was as horrible as people made me out to be...if I abused women as you say, why do so many women want so desperately to be with me?. Most of the women I have dated would give anything to get me back. I can't believe you heard such a thing and did nothing to defend me. I can't believe you thought it was true. It shows that you don't value me as a person." He went off on a tangent again, and I drifted once more. I saw his lips moving but could not fathom a word he uttered. I was too drained to respond. All I wanted was a warm bath and my bed. I managed to decipher the word "selfish" coming from Alex's lips and he had my undivided attention once more. He continued his rant....

"You kept the code for the Wi-Fi to yourself and knew I had deadlines to meet. Sometimes it's almost as if I am begging you to give me information. It's a really bad habit of yours and you need to cut it out. Another thing you need to learn to do is to say I am sorry. You are yet to apologize for your behaviour that night, and I bet you won't because you don't think you did anything wrong. What you need to learn is that it is not always about you. Sometimes it's how the other person feels about the situation; you apologize to put your partner at ease." While I agreed with that point, now was not the time I would be willing to compromise. I was hoping that he was finish, but in his usual fashion, he continued the wrath.....

"I am sick and tired of you, your negativity and your friends who you value instead of me. So you don't need to be in a relationship with me, but I will let you know that if you decide to walk out of my life, that's it. You can delete my number; I want no form of contact. So it's your call. You can let me know what you decide. Knowing you, being the selfish, caustic person you are, you don't think about anything rationally; so I think I know your answer already."

Amazing was the only word I could find to describe Alex in that moment; TRULY amazing. The more he spoke, the more I realized I didn't need him in my life. One of the lessons I have learnt is that anger reveals the underlying truth about a person. Alex communicated a mouthful, still side-stepping the issue at hand, but I appreciated him venting. I think I knew my decision. I was ready for a break in our relationship. I needed time to gather my thoughts and focus on my final exams.

I was relieved as he pulled into my driveway.

THAT ONE BITCHY FRIEND WE ALL HAVE!!!!!!!

I think Kim considered me her best friend now that we basically did everything together. Truth is, I was afraid to give someone else that title since Mia. She taught me that it was your friends that you should be more aware of than your enemies. Friends were the ones who stabbed you in the back– the ones who really had the ability to really hurt you. I wasn't sure if I could ever trust someone like that again. In all honesty, Kim was, so far, a very pleasant individual, and I assisted her with anything she needed once I could do so. I listened to her relationship issues. There was, however, this one guy I found very annoying. Kim had left him because his penis was too small even though he provided her with money. The only good thing about their relationship was that he ate her pussy extremely well. I will never forget the night she described it to me. She said he shoved his tongue so far up her vagina and licked the walls so thoroughly he could cleanse any bacteria present. This was a very twisted description but for some strange reason I found it hilarious. Maybe it was the power of her vagina, but he wouldn't leave her alone, and that annoyed the hell out of me. I blocked him from my whats app but this didn't stop him. He would use another number to message me. He was so clingy and annoying. I stopped answering messages from people who didn't identify themselves at the beginning of a conversation just for the sake of not having to deal with that asshole.

At this point in our friendship, Kim had proven herself a friend, but she was very bitchy. She didn't think things through before making decisions. She was more spontaneous than I was, and her main aim was money. She never gave me details as to how she handled her business but I knew she was the type to do anything for money, without regrets. For her, happiness meant money, brand clothing, jewellery and regular visits to the salon and nail technicians. Although we were total opposites, I found ways to adjust and work around her bitchy ways, instead of judging or arguing with her. Kim was very stubborn and had no intention to change. She was one of those persons who had to learn the hard way.

It was my last two days of freedom before final exams and I suggested to Kim that we go and party. I had not been out of the house since the quarrel with Alex. We hadn't spoken to each other since and I made sure to block him from what's app so there would be no temptations. Kim also had her plate full. Apparently she received a second warning letter from her boss. We were uncertain whether the letter was a true indication of her failure to perform on the job or revenge because she and Jemar were over. She never told me exactly what transpired, but I knew she must have really pissed him off. Jemar was a very humble person and a gentleman in my eyes. My guess was that he had found out about one of her affairs. With the way things were, we definitely needed a break. There was a beach party happening nearby, so we decided to pass through.

****

As Kim and I arrived, we passed a group of men smoking weed. I watched Kim's body tremble at the sight and smell of it. Whenever she felt stressed, weed was always her solution. I wasn't a smoker and Kim made it seem like it was a sin that I had never as much as puffed a cigar. Apparently, I was the only one she knew who didn't smoke. Her nick name for me was "miss goody two shoes" but I didn't care.

Her eyes darted across the beach as she desperately tried to find one of the weed vendors. As we went further into the crowd, we were greeted by the smell of liquor, skimpily clad women, tireless revellers who rocked, whined and gyrated to the sound of Rihanna Ft. Future's 'Love Song'. This venue had been a regular chill spot for us, so we quickly headed towards our usual spot after each grabbing a cup of vodka and cranberry. It usually only took one cup for me to hit the dance floor.

It wasn't long before I was lost in the music. I danced with my eyes closed but a few seconds later, I felt strong hands grasp my hips and pull me backwards. I didn't need to look around because I knew those hands only too well. We would always run into each other at social events. I had met him as a patient at the medical centre; while the attraction had been mutual, neither of us said anything. Instead, we acknowledged each other whenever we met at events and enjoyed each other's company. That was it. There was no telephone conversation or any form of contact outside of meeting at a social event or when he came for a check up.

I happily gyrated on his swivelling hips in time to the music. We were in complete sync on the dance floor. But then, I watched as Kim scoped out a young man with long well groomed locks and weed in hand. I watched as she braved up and approached him.

"Hey sexy, got any more weed?" she asked.

"Are you sure you can handle this babe?" he responded. "Try me," she said partially smiling. He built a spliff for her on the spot. Kim pranced around as he created her masterpiece. "Finafuckingly," she shouted, taking a gulp of vodka and lighting up the spliff. Huddled in a corner, she alternated between the pleasures of the spliff and the alcohol. It wouldn't be long before she became high. I could always tell from her smile, the redness and puffy eyes as well as her body language. Just one more puff and she would be in a different zone. The DJ kept the patrons entertained, but after three hours I started feeling a bit tired. I knew Kim just had started enjoying herself and wouldn't want to leave but I had work early in the morning.

IN LOVE WITH THE RASTA MAN

By: Bad Bitch

After Briana left, my hormones went haywire. While bracing my dancing partner against one of the columns, I slowly slid the palm of his hands over my breasts. His eyes continued to widen as I guided his hand to the secret passage under my skirt. I parted my legs slightly, never breaking eye contact, slid his fingers through my panties and led him directly to my sweet spot.

"Mmmmmmm" was all he could manage to say. "What can you do for my pussy?" I said bluntly. The shock on this stranger's face was priceless, and I must admit I never planned for those words to leave my mouth but couldn't take them back. He was stunned and I watched him silently questioning whether or not he should take up my offer. He grabbed me by the wrist, stormed across the sands and headed towards the exit. I was having a hard time keeping up with him. My legs and body felt listless. I badly needed a bed to rest. I was grateful the moment I plopped down in his car. The drive to his house was about twenty minutes.

The minute we got there, I grabbed his crotch indicating that the dick was what I wanted. There was no need for socializing and without words, he led me to the bathroom where we both stripped then stepped into the shower. We needed to wash off the sand from the party before the action began. He surprised me with the size of his dick. I didn't expect such a small dude to have such a long, thick dick. I had a deep, wide pussy that definitely needed girth and length, which by the looks of it, his big black nightstick inside of me would do the trick. He used the soap to wash my ass cheeks, letting his hands slide up and down my crack. He then paused, rinsed his dick and underneath his balls, pinned me against the wall then aimed it at my centre, ripping past my pussy lips like a bolt of thunder through a stormy sky. "Oh fuck," I grunted. "Wait, you need a condom," I managed to say breathily as I braced harder against the wall, gladly welcoming his dick. "Don't worry baby, I won't come inside you, I just have to test this pussy out first. I want to truly feel how tight and moist you are. I'll put a condom on in a minute."

My pussy stretched as he thrust in and out and I could feel him hitting my cervix. He held my waist, lifted me a bit then pulled me down hard on his dick. I loved it. Fuck the condom, I wanted his entire dick. He then pulled out, flipped me around, pushed my face against the wall, then dug so deep inside of me his dick seemed to grow another inch. As we fucked he ran his fingers in and out of my asshole then slapped my ass.

"This ass is nice. It seems like you could take a whole fist. " He then pulled out of my pussy and slowly eased his way into my ass. My body began to rock slowly back and forth as he massaged my belly and used his hands to guide my hips. I felt as light as a feather, floating back and forth. I could feel all the tension from work draining from my body. My pussy was so wet and he was swimming in it, as my walls collapsed and gave way to a river of juices. I pushed him out of me, licking and sucking my pussy juice off his dick. It tasted so good. I grabbed his cock, slid my hands up and down his shaft while I licked the head, circling it with my tongue until he spilled into my mouth. "Good girl," he said pushing his tongue into my mouth, sucking anything remaining of himself off my tongue. "You didn't spill a drop," That was good; I needed that. I could still feel my back, hips and head tingling with tiny muscular orgasms. We both headed for the bedroom and flung ourselves down on the bed. "So ummm..remind me of your name again?"

"Kimberly."

"So Kimberly, what do you do? Do you work or go to school?" he asked.

"I am a cashier, what about you?"

"I work with a cable company."

"Ok cool," I said. Cable Company didn't seem like someone who made a lot of money but I was okay for the time being.

Then there was this long awkward silence that was thankfully interrupted by my cell phone ringing. "Hey Kim, are you home safely?"

"Umm..yeah, so are you…. right?"

"Yes I have been home, but I became worried since you hadn't call which is unlike you," Briana said, sounding a little concerned.

"I am fine. I am a bit tired so I will talk to you in the morning."

"Ok sweetheart, sweet dreams."

"Same to you" immediately ending the call.

****

The next morning, I called Briana to tell her all about Andre.

"Hey Bri, whats up?"

"I am here trying to study for…." before she could finish her sentence, I spilled, "I am so in love with Andre". "Who?" Bri asked.

"The sexy rasta man from the party last night."

"In love though Kim, really? It has not been 24 hours."

"I know but I really like him, love his hair and he can fuck," I added.

"He can fuck?" Bri said flabbergasted.

"Yes. We fucked after the party and I loved it. I needed that. Bugz couldn't go more than two minutes whenever we fucked and you know it's been over between Jemar and I.

"Ok… So…..So you used a condom right."

"No I didn't, but I bought an emergency contraceptive so I will be fine," I said trying to answer Bri as quickly as possible before the detective in her took over.

She sighed before asking, "So what happens now?"

"Well he says he doesn't have a girlfriend so maybe I can give him a try. I want a rasta man in my heart," I said giggling. From the silence on the other end of the line, I knew Bri wasn't pleased and yearned to lecture me about my liberated sex life but she said nothing.

"Anyway Bri, the manager just arrived so I will call you later," I ended the call to avoid further questioning.

THE DEFINING MOMENT

By: Temptress

Four years of college seemed to have passed sooner than I anticipated. Today was the day I would be tested on just about everything; from the moment I entered nursing school, my voluntary hours and my practical. I was as nervous as a church mouse but failing was not an option. I had waited too long for this moment.

As I sat in the examination room, half hour before the scheduled start time, I tried earnestly to harness my nervousness and transform it into positive energy. I checked hundreds of times, ensuring that I had pens, pencils, erasers, white out and calculator. I even had a staple machine and mini roll of tape that only the Lord knew what I would possibly need those for, but it made me feel prepared. My legs were restless as I watched other students gradually pour into the examination room. For the first time ever I took the time out to really notice Mia. She seemed so tired. I could see the bags beneath her eyes. She even had creases along her face. She must have been really stressed. We were no longer friends, but I always knew when she had some major issues dealing with. Mia was not one to hide her problems very well. For some unexplained reason, my heart reached out to her. She looked like she needed a hug. I missed my best friend. Part of me wanted to run to her desk, hug her and wish her all the best for exams but I refrained from doing so. It's as if she felt me watching because a few seconds later she turned in my direction. Then I watched her lips formed the words "good luck" which was followed by a painful smile. I nodded and wished her the same. I turned away and focused on my shoes. I refused to look back since I knew she was still staring at me.

The first section of the exam involved matching abbreviations with their meanings. I had this section covered. Sections 2 & 3 were also manageable so I was getting into a rhythm. The next two hours of answering questions became even easier. It was a beautiful exam. My GPA had been consistently above 3.0 so I was on track to make the honour role. I was leaving this hell house with a bang. I walked out of that examination room on cloud nine. I was proud of myself.

As I rushed across the pedestrian crossing on campus, guess who stopped to let me across? The GREAT Alex himself, I was slightly happy to see him. Then again, after such a superb exam, I was happy to see just about anyone. He beckoned for me to get in the car, and I did without hesitation.

"How was the exam?" he asked.

"It was great." I responded

"You seem very happy."

"I am…I am just glad the exam was manageable because I was really worried about it."

"So what now?"" he asked.

"Now... I need food."

He laughed.

"Tell me your cravings and I will see how best I can fulfil them," he said. Those words were music to my ears really.

We headed to a nearby seafood restaurant where he ordered a cocktail and watched me devour a meal of bourbon glazed salmon.

"Not a bad choice," Alex said. "Omega 3 fatty acids in this fish have many health benefits including a protective measure against heart disease."

I couldn't have cared less about what he was saying; in fact, if the fish had cancer I didn't care. I was that hungry. We chatted for hours and naturally ended up heading back to his house afterwards. I decided to play it cool. I knew he wanted to kiss me and much more, but I made sure not to say or do anything to reveal that the feeling was mutual, so I asked him to take me home. I didn't trust myself around him.

IT JUST KIND OF HAPPENED

That night, I listened to Kim vent about how Andre was fucking other women. The same person she had fucked shortly after their first meeting. She needed to vent on a number of levels. She talked, talked and talked while I drifted in and out of sleep. At no point did she realize that it was a one way conversation. As long as she was talking about herself, that was all that mattered.

A text message came in that knocked away the sleepiness.

"I can't stop thinking about what that pussy taste like."

I didn't recognize the number so I ignored it. Another message read: "Have you ever had your pussy really sucked?"

Who the hell was sending these messages? "Let me eat your pussy please… PLEASE... Just let me satisfy my curiosity about how you taste. You don't need to do anything. Just spread your legs and let me eat you. PLEASE…"

By this time I had zoned out completely from Kim. Who the fuck was this? The nigga literally was begging to go down on me. Was he for real?

"Who is this?"

"It's Shortie," the response came back.

Shortie was the ex-boyfriend Kim insisted had a pussy vacuum for a mouth. Now he was offering to sample my goodies; the devil on my shoulder was in full command.

"How hungry are you?" I wrote back.

"I can be there in five and you will see," he answered seconds later.

"What do you think Bri?" Kim's voice crackled over the phone. I was clueless as to who or what she was asking about so I played it safe. "That's your call hon, it's all up to you."

"I knew you were going to say that." I breathed a sigh of relief and quickly ended the call.

I quickly showered and slipped into something comfortable. Before I knew it, Shortie pulled up at my gate. I had my Taser nicely positioned in the drawer of my night stand in the event he tried anything funny. As quickly as I closed the door my visitor made it clear that he had worked up an appetite, starting the tongue action right there, easing me to the floor on my back as he dug in and boy was his reputation as a master cunnilingus artist well deserved.

With his head snug between my thighs in what seemed a natural fit, Shortie wrapped his arms around my legs, threw my feet over his shoulders and started slowly. Working from the outside of my pussy, he licked it like a hungry kid with an ice-cream cone on a hot summer day. Gently working his way to the clitoris, paying keen attention to my "clitoral hood," Shortie proceeded to write the entire English alphabet in capital and common letters on my clit, with his tongue.

Then when he French kissed my genitalia bringing my labia and clit to attention and keeping them in that position, I almost broke his neck, as I suddenly clamped my legs together.

Once released, he proceeded to flick his tongue in and out with unerring accuracy, like a whip in the hands of a master – sticking, licking, sucking and brushing.

He then lightly placed his mouth and chin within my pussy, wagging it up and down or from side to side. While doing this, he spiced up the technique by letting his bottom lip hang loose rubbing against the clit. This was very enjoyable. His well shaven face meant there was no unpleasant scratching sensation of sharp facial hair as he feasted.

Then hooking his index finger in my pussy, he moved it back and forth, curling it in and out, stroking the clitoris and plumping it up so he could better access it before curling and moved the finger in a downward motion putting pressure on the anus. Both actions triggered spasms of pleasure.

His other hand briefly fondled my breast before migrating to my ass which was firmly clasped while he continued pleasuring me with his tongue. The second orgasm erupted at that point.

I was sufficiently qualified to declare that Shortie is THE BEST pussy connoisseur this side of the Milky Way. As I lay on the floor recovering from the most awesomely devastating literal tongue lashing I was ever likely to experience, I opened my eyes in time to see Shortie positioning himself to stick his fully erect three inch cock inside me. I reacted by shoving him away and when he tried again I kicked him the chest, knocking him away.

"Please babe, just give me a few seconds, that's all I need."

He got up, still pumping his dick. I backed up slowly, gearing to run for the weapon in the bedroom if need be but Shortie was done and zipping up his pants after which he angrily stormed through the door. I quickly bolted the door and stood there trembling uncontrollably. What had I been thinking? What the hell was I really thinking? I heard something scrape against the window and jumped, I was suddenly so scared. Making my way slowly towards the window I realized the noise was cause by a tree branch touching the window. I looked to make sure there was no sign of Shortie. I still could not believe I had actually done that.

BIRDS OF A FEATHER FLOCK TOGETHER

I still felt drained from that intense tongue massage last night. I remained on my back gazing at the ceiling with a partial smirk on my face. I smiled again and then it dawned on me. I had let my friends ex eat my pussy. That could never be considered betrayal or being bitchy because they were no longer together…. right? I remained silent and waited to somehow hear an answer to my rhetorical question. But all that came was the ring of my cell phone. Before I could even say hello, Kim's voice was as high pitched as ever. "Guess who came back to me last night, telling me how much he missed me?" Not giving me time to answer, she blurted out. "SHORRRTIIIIE. He volunteered to eat me as usual, we fucked after but that was whatever but the eating…OMGGASH." I felt a tad guilty listening to her talk to me about Shortie but said nothing. Last thing I needed was another scene with a friend over a man. What she doesn't know won't hurt her. That was my excuse, and I was sticking to it.

As Kim recapped her Romping Shop episode, I closed my eyes and reminisced on last night. This was such a turn on. I began to caress my nipples between my thumb and forefingers through my merino. Kim moaned louder and I got even hornier. I couldn't take it anymore. I reached between my legs with my right hand and rubbed my clit through my underwear. I kept my ears trained to Kim's voice and every word she uttered. I started gasping for breath and tried to refrain from moaning. I slid my underwear to the side with one hand. I found my own wetness and started furiously rubbing myself, getting lost in my own fantasy world as Shortie did sensual things to my body. I palmed my left breast with my free hand. Soon, I could feel cum trickling down onto my fingertips. Now I let myself moan. I came like I never had before, forgetting all about Kim on the line… "Holllly fuck did you just cum" she asked. I felt a little embarrassed so I remained quiet. "This is so frigging sexy. My story turned you on. O my gosh," she laughed then continued speaking. "What exactly turned you on? Was it me or my story? Maybe I could let you in on one of my threesomes. She thought I was into women. If only she knew what really turned me on. I laughed once more. "So silence means consent Bri?"

"I am going to get ready for work. Talk to you later Kim, have a great day." I didn't know what was happening but I was still horny as hell. Oh fuck it, I needed a good dick right now, so I called in sick then called Alex.

MAKE UP SEX?

He placed a serviette to the corner of my lip, gently dabbing some strawberry juice and this simple action made my legs quiver. He smiled deliciously while offering the plate as if fully aware of the intentions of my body.

Feeling his bulge I gently unbuckled his pants, lowered myself and let my tongue work. Alex groaned loudly, and I knew he was close to climaxing. I felt the throbbing before the explosion that almost landed in my mouth. At the last second, I pulled away, still maintaining my grip on his balls. I made sure he climaxed because I was so fucking horny. His breathing was still heavy, but he managed to muster enough energy to take me to the television room where he tossed me on the couch, flung himself on top then buried himself inside of me. Seconds later I climaxed as Alex did.

I cried softly inside as he stroked my head. Alex was such a complex person but somehow I still wanted him badly.

TWITTER.....OOMF (ONE OF MY FOLLOWERS)

I called in sick the next day, using up my last sick day, opting to stay home and be a bum. I did absolutely nothing of importance. The whole day I alternated from Twitter, Facebook, Instagram, just about every social network.

One of my followers on twitter retweeted a post by one of her followers which I found very hilarious. The conversation between the two girls was so entertaining that I decided to send a follow request to the one my follower constantly retweeted. As soon as she accepted, I immediately enlarged her profile picture. I held my breath for a few seconds at the sight of the display pic. I knew that face. That pink lipstick and a pierced tongue were her trademark. My first encounter with that face was that time I sign in to my email account on Alex's computer. She had the same display pic being used on her gmail account. The next encounter with that face wearing the same bright coloured lipstick was in a picture I accidentally viewed, which showed her widely welcoming Alex's dick. It wasn't long before she began mentioning me or retweeted almost every other tweet. She made me laugh and kept me entertained. Then we began communicating via direct messages rather than mentions.

Did you know me before meeting me on twitter?

No, I responded

So why did you decide to follow me? Read another DM.

"Marsha kept retweeting your posts plus I found the conversation between both of you very entertaining and to top it off, you are cute. So I decided to follow you, " I responded.

You are cute too and sexy. She hash tagged "no homo" in her response.

"I never said you were but confession is good," I responded, laughing to myself.

"Heh..Well maybe bi not homo...Did I say that out loud....Ok I am done", she texted back.

"It's neither here nor there to me," I responded.

"That's good to know," she responded.

We conversed for hours until we finally decided to exchange numbers then our conversation continued on whats app messenger.

"Do you know Alex?" The text read.

"I know several Alex. You have to be more specific," I responded.

"Alex Latouche?" She stated.

I stared at the cell phone for a few minutes before responding; uncertain as to how to respond.

"Yes I know Alex Latouche. He is my ex-boyfriend," I responded.

Oh…How long ago was that?

Maybe a month or two… I responded.

"What happened between you two, if you don't mind sharing?" Another text read.

"I don't know. I just got bored and wanted new dick," I responded.

"LMAAO," she texted back.

"I didn't know you two weren't together because he still talks about you," she said.

"Well I am glad I had an impact," I stated.

There were so many things running through my mind, but I didn't want to mess up the flow of things so I waited and let her lead the conversation instead.

"So are you his woman now?" I asked.

"It's complicated. We have been on and off but no matter what I can't leave him. I am whipped by that dick. I know he doesn't care about me the way he does you but the sex is good, lool."

"LOOL, are you serious? So your relationship with him is just sex and you are ok with that?" I asked.

"Not really but he is all I have. He is what I know. Met him as a teenager and he paid my college tuition, took care of the bills, helped my mother with whatever we needed, so I just feel like I owe him everything. I finished college and was unable to get a job and he was the one who got me something. He continuously helped me through hard times. I don't know what I would do without him," she said. I sympathized with her situation but, I wasn't going to allow anyone to have that much dominion over me..

"While I do understand that he provides for you, that doesn't mean you should let him take advantage of you. You said it yourself that you don't think he cares as much about you. But you don't have to put up with that and agree with him to run around with other women. That is unfair to you." I said.

"Sigh. I know but……" she was hesitant to continue, but she finally did....

"I am getting money. I am not happy but he takes care of me," another text read a few seconds later. What was with these women and money? There was no way I could KNOWINGLY have sex with someone who was also sleeping around and be ok with it just because he had money. I couldn't understand how Kim did it and sure as hell couldn't understand how she did, especially knowing about the other women. To the point where he discussed the other woman with you? Who the hell does that?

"So…ummm. What does he say when he mentions me to you. I am curious?" I texted back and eagerly anticipated a response.

"It's mainly when we fuck," she responded.

"What the hell?" I texted back instantly.

"He called your name or spoke dirty, telling me what he would do to you and this turned him on even more. I found it sexy as well to be honest. I am a squirter and I hear you drip and really wet the sheets all the time. Can you imagine if we combined for a threesome? You know he badly wants that right? Would you do something like that?" I could tell by she was excited by the thought of a threesome with me. This is where I should have ended the conversation, but I was somewhat curious – I must admit.

I read the message about fifty times before responding. Me???? Threesome??? With the other girl being someone I clearly have been cheated on with? This must be Karma. She seemed so comfortable with it all. Was I to be flattered by the fact that he is thinking about me or calling my name while fucking her?

After five minutes she sent another text. "Helllllerrr…."

"Nah threesomes are not my thing. Besides I have never kissed a girl not to mention I don't know the first thing about eating pussy. So that would be a very LAME threesome."

"I can teach you……" she said. I couldn't help but laugh. I admired her openness with her sexuality.

"You are crazy…"I texted back. Shelly and I conversed the whole day. She said talking to me made her horny, so she was going to call Alex.

Enjoy…I replied. Just to make sure, I texted her to find out when she was about to leave and as soon as she told me she did, I called Alex.

"I miss you and I am very horny right now," I said.

"Really," he said then pausing for a little while. "I have a meeting so I will let you know the plan after." He continued. That's all I needed to hear. "Ok" I said, fucking liar.

That night Shelly filled me in on every detail of the night with Alex and for some strange reason I didn't hate her. I was dangerously mad at Alex but not her.

ANOTHER WOMAN'S STAND POINT

In time, Shelly and I became closer. I think I spoke to her more often during the days than I did with Alex. I considered her naïve but nice. She told me stories upon stories about her experiences with Alex. I observed him drowning in his lies trying to juggle both of us and I played along.

I remember seeing multiple text messages at one point with her name constantly popping up on the cell phone, so I asked and he said she was an ex. I was TOTALLY AMAZED…The blatant lie was unbelievable especially since they had fucked only couple hours before and he had dropped her home before coming for me.

I continued to play the cards in his favour. When I wasn't busy with work, I was having my period or I had family engagements but it didn't bother him as much because he had old faithful Shelly.

WHEN STRANGERS COME TOGETHER

I was finally going to meet his sex friend. I was a bit apprehensive but wanted to find out more about Alex and it seemed the best way to do so was through her. The time to meet Shelly came by quicker than expected. I had been so immersed in business I lost track of the time and would be late.

When I finally arrived, I watched her seated at the bar and approached slowly, not wanting to frighten her.

"Hi Shelly," I said smiling.

"Hi, finally you are here," she responded.

Her eyes were fixed on me, while she bit her lips. I hated when people stared at me and I didn't know what they were thinking.

"So shall we order?" I said, trying to lighten the mood.

"That sounds like a great idea. I am starving." Truth is, I didn't have much of an appetite and it felt slightly awkward meeting with her knowing that she routinely fucked Alex. I wasn't sure what Shelly and I would discuss, but I tried to remain cool.

"I'll have a sweet thigh chilli wings with mash potatoes and a glass of sex on the beach," I told the waitress. Shelly ordered a cheese burger special with French fries and cranberry. After the waitress left with our orders there was a brief moment of silence.

"So how was the exam? How long do you have to wait for the results?" she asked. "About one week. I can't wait to officially finish even though I don't have a job lined up."

"Well I am sure you can always work at one of Alex's medical practices. After all you did some voluntary hours last summer. So you should be familiar with how they operate"

How did she know this, had Alex discussed me? Why would he do such a thing?

"I don't think so. I heard he doesn't treat his staff well?"

"Gosh, are you serious?" Shelly asked sounding slightly surprised.

"So I have heard."

"I guess if you offer favours maybe you will be treated nicely, who knows maybe even get a salary increase." She and I both laughed.

"You can get anything from Alex with sex. He loves it too much," she continued.

"You know that better than anyone," I said as I smiled.

"Yes I do. Girl, I am whipped by that dick." I think Shelly was settled and ready to talk. I watched as she shifted in her seat and loosened her hair a bit. I must admit that she had very luscious lips; they looked kissable. The thought of kissing a girl had crossed my mind a few times and for a brief moment Shelly seemed ideal to experiment with. After all, we both found each other attractive, but then I remembered Alex had mentioned to me several times that he didn't kiss her. I didn't believe him but if he was fucking her for years and still wouldn't kiss her, then why should I?

I was drawn back to reality by Shelly's voice, "He is so jealous, insecure and controlling but I love him." I couldn't help but sympathize with her. Money and the material things were obviously clouding her judgment. Based on our conversation over the past weeks, I gathered their relationship was based on transactional sex. He knew her weakness and used it. Whenever they fussed he would take her shopping, to hotels and give her money to purchase the Remi and Brazilian hair she loved to wear that he would often times complain about her wasting money on a regular day. He had her wrapped around his fingers, but she was too caught up to realize that.

Poor soul, I thought. "So what do you really expect Shelly? A man is going to spend on you constantly, fly you around the world and not want to control you? Life would be perfect if men were made like that." We both laughed.

"Stop acting as if you've never accepted these fancy offers when you were with him"

"No I haven't actually. I don't take things from him neither do I ask him for anything and I certainly haven't left the country with him" She scrutinized me after I said that. I could tell she was trying to figure out whether I was lying.

"Well you are independent, but I on the other hand would love to be kept. I know he will eventually buy me a car or a house."

"And you will forever be controlled and treated like his investment, so don't complain," I shot back.

The waitress returned with the meals. I was glad for the food as this eased the tension I had just created. She bit into her burger then managed to utter, "I see why he likes you. You are independent, ambitious, smart, sexy and beautiful."

"You shouldn't compare yourself to others," I said. "You are fine with that ass. Two huge racks of breasts and a lovely ass," I added. "Alex should love fucking you from the rear."

"OMG, Briana," she choked. "I can't believe you said that. Here I was thinking that you were a church girl."

"You know it's the truth," I ignored her. "An ass like that is perfect for doggy style." She grinned from ear to ear and continued eating.

"You haven't touched your food," she said.

"I am not really hungry," I said. It wasn't long before she started spilling information again. Gosh she had lots to say about Alex. There were quite a few shocking revelations, but I was mentally making my notes. She was giving me exactly what I needed. Actually, the night turned out better than I had anticipated.

PUTTING THE PIECES TOGETHER

After dinner with Shelly, my mind was very uneasy. I had finally gotten closure, and it was too much to bear. I laid on the bed listless with my eyes fixed on the ceiling, as I reminisced on my journey with Alex. All the lies he told me replayed like a movie in my head now that I had the missing pieces.

Let's start with the baby shower incident. Alex made plans for us to travel out of town to spend the day at the beach. Unfortunately, my friend had her baby shower on the same day. I figured I could always make it up to her if she became upset with me about missing such a precious event for her. On the other hand, if I cancelled on Alex, it would have been misery for days. So I opted to miss the baby shower. It wasn't until I was dressed and waiting for an hour that he text to say that he wouldn't be able to make it. He had some last minute business to handle. Checking into a hotel with Shelly was the last minute business he had to handle.

There was another incident where he picked Kim and I up from a beach party; as we departed, a woman called to him. The look on his face was as if he was the witness to a crime. I remember the woman saying she didn't know he attended these types of events. He ignored her and drove off speedily. Low and behold, Shelly was supposed to attend that beach event but had changed her mind. However, her friend Natalie, who also happened to be someone he fucked or was still fucking at that time, was there and she was the one who called to him. Alex had been lying to both of us for quite a while. Juggling multiple women seemed to have been his routine for years.

My mind then fast forwarded to the time I borrowed his laptop. My eyes caught the cover of a folder that had a naked woman but was entitled 'class work'. Of course, this sparked my curiosity. The folder contained pictures of an orgy. The women were all middle aged and some of them were inserting bananas, bottles and broomsticks. I cringed and wondered why the folder had been entitled 'class work' to begin with. Viewing that one photo album made me want to view more. So I opened the pictures folder.

I saw pictures of who I now know to be Shelly. Posing in lingerie, naked, pictures of her in compromising positions, pictures of her clit, there were pictures of her kissing other women at what seemed like a college campus and multiple pictures with Alex's dick in her mouth. There was also a video of them having sex.

Even though I had seen these pictures back then, I shrugged off all the evidence. At the time, I didn't care as much about Alex for those things to have bothered me. But as we got to know each other and ended up being together, the images resurfaced and the uncertainties lingered. But I foolishly disregarded everything after convincing myself that these were from the past. I didn't believe in digging up things from the past either, so I left it at that. But then my gut feeling told me otherwise. Although my inner voice told me something was not right, I still clung to him to make things work. Maybe I wasn't different from Shelly after all. I knew about his skeletons, yet I still gave in to his pursuits. Now, here I was fraternizing with the woman he fucked every chance he got, after lying to her about him being my ex and at the same time I said nothing to him about finding out about her. I kept everything to myself and worked with it, but not anymore. Truly, I was disgusted.

I rolled over and buried my face in the pillows. Incidents of the past leading up to the present bombarded my mind. The many accusations Alex made about me cheating when we drifted apart, when really he was the one who had been guilty of such acts. I laid in bed for hours thinking.

I was unsure as to whether I could ever trust Alex again. Some people would say that everyone deserved a second chance. But to me, someone is not deserving of second or third chances unless they learn from their mistakes. Not Alex. Good sex and companionship was all he wanted from women. He was his own king. I soon came to the realization that he didn't see the need for any obligations to anyone at this point in his life.

However, I learnt a few things from all this drama:

1) Without communication there is no relationship.

2) Without respect, there is no love;

3) Without trust, there is no reason to continue;

4) Always trust your gut instincts. If you genuinely feel something is wrong, then it usually is;

5) Being single, you should try to focus on being a better you instead of looking for someone better than your ex, because a better you will attract a better next.

I was ready to clear Alex Latouche from my system once and for all. I won't deny the fact that we had great times together, but it was time to move forward. The pieces finally fit and the puzzle now made sense. I was finally letting go.

IT'S OVER!!!

Today was not the most appropriate day to end the relationship, as it was Alex's birthday. He had been calling and texting all week, sharing his plans for spending the day with me. Even though I really wanted him to have a good birthday, I wasn't going to be the one he spent it with. I didn't want to be around him, but he wouldn't take no for an answer. He called and texted, and I ignored him until I finally blurted it out and told him that it was over. Clearly, that became motivation for him to step up his advances, because, a few minutes later, a text message came in that read: "I am coming to pick you up from work."

I guess he didn't take me seriously. He continued to call and text, but I ignored him. One hour later another text read:

"I agree with you. You don't need to be in a relationship with me, it's not worth it. I am not really a friend of yours. You have your allegiances elsewhere and I am sure you have good reasons for that. You keep it up. I hope you are very happy that I will not be celebrating my birthday any at all because of you. Yes you will say I blame you for this but I could have made other plans but no, I wanted to spend the day with you, as you made me happy and look at this now. I am noting all this. I hope you won't be surprised at some point when you possibly need me the most and what my response will be. No worries, it's all good. And you don't need to reply, as it will be something feisty from you. You are not really a friend."

I ignored the message and continued to clean up my work station but they kept coming. When he wasn't calling me selfish, I apparently lacked humility and understanding. He texted and texted and vented and called me names even more. Out of my growing frustration I responded.

"Ok. You have said it all, so why do you keep texting me. You claim I am selfish, stubborn, lack humility and character and think the world revolves around me. I mean you no good and want nothing but to drive you and your business under the ground. So knowing all this, why the hell do you keep texting me? Leave this horrible person alone and live your frivolous life. Channel your time and energy into someone else who possesses all the qualities that I lack; someone like Shelly McIntosh. I am not interested in you Mr Latouche. I am DONE. So continue to text and bash me all you want. Go ahead and vent, call me every name you can think of if it makes you feel better. "

After I sent him that message, he didn't reply for a few hours. I knew mentioning Shelly in the text must have hit hard. The son of a bitch must be trying to figure out how the hell I knew about her. Just as I thought the messages had ended, in came another one...

"If you were humble and meant me good, you would put all that behind you and prove me wrong. But you are one person who don't back down. You of all persons should know when to. It's a trait you need to develop. You may be right in most situations but for peace sake and being appreciative of someone, you take the other road instead. But guess what, even after all I have done for you, you would never do that for me. I was really hoping you would have surprised me."

Twenty minutes later, I received another text message. "My birthday will be unhappy, thanks to you. I hope you feel good, as you only see your side. Once you are satisfied with what you do, that's all you really care about."

I wondered how long before he would stop venting. It was always amazing how men reacted when a woman decided that she would no longer tolerate the bullshit. Just by the way Alex reacted you would think I was the problematic partner. LOYAL, was all I was to him but he could never say the same. Even when I knew of his affairs, the pictures, the videos, the accidental text messages, voice notes, stumbled over women's underwear under his bed, I stuck with him. For what reason…only the Lord knew. Now the bastard had the audacity to tell me to turn a blind eye to certain things for a peaceful life. I had been doing that all this time. Alex on the other hand was clearly complacent with his bad habits. But it didn't matter anymore. He was free to do whatever he pleased.

Later that evening, still another text message– he decided to up the ante: "A car was going to be your gift for graduation but I was waiting for the right time to give it to you. I was tempted so many times to give it to you before but was waiting for the right time. I choose to say it now, not because I want you to be anything to me but just for you to know. I will go tomorrow and cancel it, thank you. No reply is necessary."

I laughed. This stunt would have probably worked with Shelly. He knew I wasn't a materialistic person either so I don't know why he would even try that. I supposed he thought because it was A CAR we were talking about, I would have made an exception. As much as I wanted one, I wasn't about to accept one under such circumstance. In a few days I would become a registered nurse and finally be able to enjoy that long awaited pay increase. Buying a car was also something that would happen eventually. I was in no rush.

I was very thankful for meeting Shelly. As a woman, another woman isn't always necessarily your enemy. You may gain some insight as to who someone really is from someone else's view point. I think Alex just turned me the fuck off from men in general. I had never been lied to and cheated on as badly before until I met Alex. So now my new mind set was:

Sex is a business that is not to be compromised or jeopardized by incompetence, ignorance and especially not STDs.

Love is a virus. It's a deceptive virus that works in conjunction with the object of your affection and when it dissipates, infidelity is the end result.

I would never allow myself to be taken for granted by another man in this lifetime. I was done playing the nice girl. I called myself the Temptress. I knew how to flirt, and I intended to use this to my advantage to the best of my ability. Get in, get what I want, then get out but play it safe.

For a moment I had a fleeting idea, maybe I should just pretend to be back with Alex and then take the motherfucker's car. I quickly dismissed the thought and got back to my new mindset. Fuck him!

HORNY FOR MONEY

By: Bad Bitch

I needed money badly. I really needed to go shopping at my friend's boutique especially since she was expecting new arrivals this weekend. Clothes, shoes, accessories, a manicure and pedicure were a few of the things on my list. Even though I received my salary two days ago, I was broke, since the bulk of my money was geared towards settling my previous bill at the boutique. The cocaine business that I got involved in with Bugz had a few glitches, so the influx was not as steady and was not producing the lump sum it usually did. Jemar was also being a bitch about the stupid Mathematics and English courses he paid for, demanding that I compensate him for the examination fees since I deliberately didn't show up. I shouldn't have to pay him back for shit because I told him I didn't want to go school and he insisted. I had about one week left to work as a cashier. Then, to top it all off, my parents insisted I pay my share of the utility bills.

I couldn't see why I had to contribute to the damn bills on a salary barely above minimum wage. I could have bought the chevron handbag and a pair of earrings with the money I gave them.

The biggest party of the summer would be held this weekend and I HAD to be there. I also had to make a fashion statement, so I needed a good amount of money.

As I watched the customers browse the store, my mind raced through my telephone contacts thinking of possible men I could get cash from on such short notice. Money doesn't stay with me very long, so I was always in need. I had only one option. I had met this guy on Facebook about a week ago. He was about 20 years older, but I didn't care. It was all about the Benjamin's. I was about to lose my mind if not even a hundred dollar bill came my way. I quickly called him up and finally agreed to meet him in person. I told him that we should meet for lunch today. This was perfect. I was determined to save every penny towards my shopping spree, so a sandwich biscuit and orange juice was all I budgeted for today's lunch. So Mr. Facebook saved me from starvation.

****

I don't know if it was because I had not eaten all day why the food tasted so delicious. I had two juicy miniature beef burgers with bacon, perfectly grilled and served on sliced French baguettes with caramelized onion, grilled mushroom and Swiss cheese. I was not fond of his company but certainly enjoyed my lunch. I don't know how young girls dated men who were more than 10 years older because I was disgusted just to sit here with him. I felt like everyone was staring at us, but I had one thing on my agenda.

"I have 20 minutes to spare and this drink is making me horny. Do you have any solutions to my problem?" I asked, staring pointedly at him. The slight grin I got in return told me I was on the right track. Nothing conquered the power of the pussy. He took me to his home, no questions asked. Numerous portraits of what seemed to be his wife and children were strategically placed on the wall of the hallway that led to the staircase. I was going to fuck him in the master bedroom and make him remember it each time he made love to his wife. I hastily unbuckled his belt, unzipped his pants and pulled them down. He was already throbbing and eagerly awaiting my warm tongue. I had a tight grip on his legs, pulling him towards me as I guided his dick into my warm mouth. "Oh shit," he screamed and that was before I drew him into my throat and held him there with just the power of mouth. No lips, just throat. No hands just my hot mouth receiving him. There was no sucking, just deep mouth-fucking. So unexpected, so aggressive, that in a few minutes he was on the verge of climaxing. He pulled out of my mouth, lifted and slammed me down unto his dick and with just a few more thrusts into my pussy spilled his cum. That was not even five minutes, but it was a perfect quickie.

"Damn. You suck dick very well. I have tried so many times to get Andrea to do it but she just won't. Sometimes I have to pay for that shit to be done."

That was my cue.

"Well you can do me a favour and compensate me in cash for taking your dick out of misery. You can always pay me to suck it. Just tell me when and where." He laughed, looking down at me but I held a straight face.

"I need $15, 000 to help my parents cover the bills."

"Sweetheart, I can't give you that amount. You are not my woman."

"Whatever," I said angrily as I dressed. This son of a bitch was being so cheap. He could more than afford $15,000.

"Take me back to work," I said bitchily.

"Babe, come on, why are you acting like this?"

"Don't babe me," I shot back. "I need to get back to work, so let's go."

"Ok," he said, searching for the keys to his BMW seven series yet he couldn't fucking give me $15,000. He had wasted my damn time, and I also wasted a perfectly great deep throat for NOTHING; I was pissed. I was desperate for money and it seemed like for the first time in history my pussy had failed me.

****

When we arrived at my workplace he bent over to kiss me but I shoved him off. I stepped out of the car and slammed the door behind me. "Kim, Kim," I heard him calling but I continued walking. "Ok, I guess you won't need this again." Those words stopped me dead in my tracks. I peered over my shoulder and saw his arms stretched out with an envelope. I approached slowly and grabbed it from him.

"I was just messing with you but you showed how much of a money hungry bitch you are."

"Now are you going to give me that kiss I asked kindly for?" I smiled then leaned closer and allowed him to shove his tongue into my mouth. It was a very wet and sloppy kiss. He was a three minute man who couldn't even deliver a proper kiss. "So you will call me later?" he asked, beginning to sound a bit clingy already.

"Yes I will. Thanks again." I rushed inside the bathroom to see if the full amount of $15,000 was there and screamed when I counted $30,000. I looked at myself in the mirror. The power of the pussy, I said patting it gently. I was set for the weekend.

BUMP INVASION

By: Bad Bitch

I had a great time. I invited Briana, but she had been under the weather since her ordeal with Alex.

However, I was having a few issues myself. I found that I was constantly nauseous and the smell of just about anything made me throw up. Whenever I brushed my teeth, the mint in the toothpaste caused me to vomit a few times. After a sip of water at work I was so nauseated I had to rush to the ladies room. I purchased a pregnancy test kit at the end of my shift. I burst through the doors of my home and headed straight to the bathroom and bombarded the plastic stick with my hot and strong urine. I shook the stick, fidgeted, shook and anxiously awaited the results. One stripe, what a relief!

After my fourth pregnancy scare, I decided it was time to take a break from sex for a while. I was taking a long break. Whenever I craved the dick I watched porn and masturbated or if I was at work, slipped in my bullet and had the best five minutes of my life in the ladies room. However, a few days the skin of my pussy became inflamed and hot to the touch, and I could not scratch enough to soothe the powerful itch. I damped my rag with warm water and placed it on my vagina, hoping it would soothe the itching, but it didn't. So I visited the doctor.

I watched as the doc put on his gloves and lubricated his fingers. He reached inside of me with one hand then with his other, pressed around on my stomach. He reached even deeper inside, tapping and searching around for lumps, bumps or anything unusual. The doc then pulled out his hand then told me to relax. I guess he sensed this was my first pelvic examination/pap smear. A minute later, a cold speculum slipped inside of me, then the swipe of dry cotton, a pinch, a squeeze then another swipe and it was over. I exhaled then relaxed my pelvis then the rest of my body. "All I need is something to control the itching, right Doc?" After dropping the gloves in the trash receptacle, he turned to look at me. "Let's await the test results. In the meantime, minimize sexual activities."

"I haven't done anything in almost two weeks," I said with a slight grin but he held a straight face. I was pretty sure the bumps were nothing. They had dried up and disappeared without leaving scars. I tried calling Facebook guy, but he hadn't returned any of my calls.

After two weeks, I went back to my doctor for the results which confirmed genital herpes.

I didn't know what to do or where to go from here. I have had a few wild encounters but I had been ok prior to fucking with Facebook guy and figured I must have gotten that from him. I called his phone a million times, left messages and still there was no answer.

At home I cried all night...tears of anger and tears of pity. I called him again only to hear a message that incoming calls to the number had been restricted. I cried even more. No wonder the bastard gave me more than the $15,000 I had requested, knowing fully well that I had sucked and fucked his herpes-infested dick. I cried until my stomach hurt, my body convulsed and shook. I cried until my crying was merely a noise my mouth made and no more tears would come. I cried until I fell asleep.

A MAN WILL SAY ANYTHING

By: Temptress

Alex and I hadn't spoken for about a month. I thought about him occasionally and often wondered if he was ok but made no attempt to contact him, and he didn't either until today. I was surprised when his name came up on the phone, and I answered without giving it much thought.

"Can you come outside?" I peeped through the window hesitant at first but eventually went out to him. I took a long, deep breath before opening the car door.

"Hello maam, how are you?"

"I am fine thanks and you?"

"Miserable. I miss you."

I rolled my eyes. "What do you want Alex? Why are you here?"

"We need to talk Briana. I don't want to lose you. I miss you terribly."

"There is nothing to talk about," I scoffed.

"What do you want to know? I will tell you everything. I need you Briana and have been miserable-well more miserable since you left. Do you want to know about Shelly; it's nothing serious. We have great sex and she does whatever I tell her to; all the freaky things I like. So I like her for that. She is not someone I would ever settle with. There is no form of intimacy. We don't cuddle, I don't kiss her. I don't take her out with my friends. All these things I do with you. Since you two are now friends you can ask her. I don't do any of those things with her. If she says I do, that's a lie. As God liveth Briana, I am telling you I don't view her like that."

Somehow I found this hard to believe. I remained silent. "Shelly would give anything to get me to cuddle and profess my love to her, as I do to you but she is not who I want."

He thought this was JUST about Shelly? This was about the many lies, the many times he cancelled on me for a booty call. This was about his seemingly frivolous sex life. Most importantly, the five year relationship he had with a gynaecologist who was also employed in his business, that he claimed was over. He had me, the gynaecologist and Shelly all at once. So should I put all this on the table? Should I really whip out the names of all his victims? Should I really mention every incident and lie he told me? No, I didn't think I needed to. I didn't have the time for that. I wasn't going down that road. So I remained silent and allowed the anger to seep through my skin.

"Bri, I am really sorry. I know I haven't been the best of persons and have put you through a lot and I deserve every bit of attitude or hatred you have for me but I am asking you please to forgive me. Don't give up on me yet. I promise I will make this right. List your demands, make your rules, I will do them– every single one. You are all I need Briana. You make me happy. When I am without you, I am so miserable. I am not getting any younger, so I think it's time I get my act together and settle down."

I wanted to believe that he would do things differently if I gave him a second chance, but there was that part of me that didn't. I still cared deeply for him, but he had breached my trust too many times.

"Briana, can you look at me? Do I disgust you that much?"

I wanted to say yes so badly, but didn't. I continued looking through the window.

"You are rare. You are a good woman and I am not giving up so easily. You are the first young woman I have dated who is not interested in me because of what I may be able to provide. You are independent, focused, you know what you want and I like that. I want us to start over and work things out. I want you to come and live with me. I want you Briana. I need you. I mean every word. I am weak for you and will do whatever it takes to keep you. I will commit to you only."

I could feel the lump in my throat growing as I fought the tears. Why was he saying all these nice things? Why wouldn't he leave me alone? This was too much.

"I don't beg people but I am BEGGING you babe because I NEED you and only you. I promise I will be different. Let's not lose this please, it's precious and genuine. Could you please say something? Could you at least look at me?"

I turned to look at him with tears welled up in my eyes, and without responding I said very curtly, "I am going back inside now". He attempted to hug me, but I shoved him off. This was too much. I left the vehicle and headed back inside without looking back.

I rolled myself into a ball and cried myself to sleep.

BRIBE OR GENEROSITY?

"I don't get how these people claim to be sick yet they would wait the whole day for a particular doctor to come in. If you are really sick wouldn't you try to get treatment from whoever is on duty? Or am I old school?" Niela said to me. She was the eldest nurse at the medical centre and had been there for over 15 years.

"Do you really want me to answer the part about you being old school?" I asked. She threw a pair of gloves at me for saying that.

"How are you doing really?" Niela asked as she searched through the cabinet for a patient's docket.

"I'm okay."

"Don't worry about Alex. He is an idiot for hurting you the way he did."

Her words brought back memories of how he had begged me for my forgiveness yesterday.

"Life…You live and learn," I said. "I will be fine."

"Ummm, Bri," Neila said pointing towards the monitor. I watched as Alex strolled into the doctor's office with his fine self.

"What are you doing here?"

"There is more we need to discuss," he said.

"Really, like what?" I said furiously.

"I didn't come here to argue. Do you have a minute to talk? I won't keep you long."

"Niela, can you give me five minutes please? I said as I got up from behind the desk and stepped outside.

"I came here to apologize to you Briana. I am really sorry."

"Didn't you do enough of that yesterday?" I asked.

"I didn't just come for that, another reason is that I would like to buy you a car."

"You are amazing." I said as I turned away from him.

"Can you at least hear me out," he said, grabbing my arms.

"Our relationship didn't work but I want to know that you are comfortable. You will officially be a nurse in a few days, which will mean longer shifts, late nights and public transportation can be difficult at times. Also, if you don't already have a job lined up when you are finished, you are welcome to work with me"

"I appreciate your concern Alex but no thank you," I said.

"Could you please stop being stubborn for once and let me do something nice for you. At least think carefully about it? That's all I ask." I headed back inside.

"Briana, are you ok?" Niela asked.

"Yes I am fine."

"Good because it's going to be a long day. We have a mob of angry patients in the waiting area and a doctor who is moving like a slug." We both laughed.

I took an additional 5 minute break to call Kim. "Hey mama, what's good?" she answered.

"Alex offered to buy me a car but I think I am going to turn him down," I said still thinking about whether I was making the right decision.

"Now why the hell would you do that?" she said

"I don't want anything from him."

"I know you are used to buying things for yourself but if Alex wants to buy you a car, let him do it and don't settle for just anything. Get something you really want."

"I don't know Kim. I don't feel right doing this. I need to pray about it."

"Prayer is good but in this situation, you need to use some common sense. You don't want to be taking the bus all your life."

"I hope it doesn't come to that but I have been saving so I should have enough money in another year or two for a down payment...." I said

"Or you can let Alex help you," Kim interjected.

"I'll think about it."

"You are crazy, Briana. I don't know what there is to think about. The man is rich. He can buy you an entire island, but no you prefer to live in a shoebox and take the bus. I thought I trained you right but…"

"Ok. Ok. Ok. I will meet with Alex and cement the details. I needed to ensure that this was not just a bribe. I will make sure I have something in writing too."

"Now that's my girl."

"Anyway, I have to get back to work. Talk to you later."

THE AFTERMATH

By: Bad Bitch

Bri was lucky. All I ever wanted was to have nice things, travel and just enjoy life. I fought and worked so hard to earn what she seemed to be getting effortlessly. Just like that, a man desired to buy her a car and she was refusing it. I probably would have had to suck many dicks and be fucked in all my openings before a man offered me something like that. The one time I got 30 grand in one sitting, herpes came with it. The one time I found a man who cared for me deeply and wanted to help me better myself and mould me into the woman of his dreams, he became intimidated by my past and left my sorry ass. My three months of filling in as a cashier had come to an end. Bugz's drugs and gun trade was on a hold because police were snooping around too much, and so I was left with nothing. My life was pathetic. I was a pathetic individual who had no qualifications, no job, no man, no car, no house or apartment after all my hard work. Instead, I was left with herpes. I cried all over again. Might as well I had gotten AIDS, I would die a quicker less painful death. Living like this, was the worst thing ever. What was left for me to look forward to? What else could possibly be destined for me? What was I supposed to do now?

By: Temptress

I passed my exam as expected and made the honour roll. I didn't attend the graduation ceremony. I didn't see the point. I had no boyfriend or any other close friend to share the moment with. Yes I had Kim, but I didn't see the need to pay thousands of dollars to wear a gown just for her. We could always celebrate together at a later date. I accepted an offer I received in the public sector and would do sessions at private establishments on weekends or in the evenings. I was making good money, so I had no complaints.

As for my social life, Kim and I remained as friends. She became a little withdrawn and no longer shared her sexual escapades with me. Something was not right, but I wasn't about to nag her about it. If she wanted me to know, she would have said something. Whatever the issue was, I hope she managed to resolve it successfully. Shelly and I didn't talk as often anymore. I didn't hate her, but distanced myself because she was a constant reminder of Alex and the struggle he put me through. I never spoke to Mia again either. However, David and I speak on special occasions – birthdays, Easter and Christmas. I dated a few guys, but there was nothing serious. I didn't see myself falling for another man anytime soon. Furthermore, I was too focussed on my career.

As for Mr Alex Latouche, we kept our distance. There was no communication other than when we met at conferences, health fairs or other work-related events. He fulfilled his part of the bargain and got me a shiny red Honda civic. He handled the payment and insurance coverage of the vehicle and the title was also in my name. So far, he had kept his word, but I prepared for the worst regardless. If ever he decided to use the vehicle as an excuse to involve me somehow, that would be the day I willingly parked it at his gate and left it even though it was in my name. Aside from that minor Alex-related concern, life was good.

Epilogue

Kimberly eventually came out of her depressive state and gave life a third attempt. She accepted the treatment for her STI and has not had sex since. As a food connoisseur, she was also a good cook, so she utilized her cooking skills and volunteered to assist in the preparation of the meals for her mother's church for their outings or community treats for the kids until she was offered a permanent job as the chef at the church. She prepared meals for the basic school owned by the church as well as any other functions they organized – church camp, conventions, youth week etc. On weekends she would prepare soup and chicken and chips at home as a means of earning a little extra income. As it related to her social life, she dated one of the musicians in the church. She was not baptized but has been going to church more often with her mother and new admirer. She was motivated to attend services and remained very close friends with Briana.

As for Briana, she continued along the academic path. She was rewarded nurse of the year in the hospital she worked. After a year and sixth months, she went back to school to pursue a course in midwifery. She became a member of a well-known charity organization and assisted primarily with the health and development of children. Alex was history, but she remained single in the fully furnished two-bedroom house she purchased. Her sexual needs were often times satisfied by a collection of sex toys, and she still believed firmly that: Sex is a business not to be compromised or jeopardized by incompetence, ignorance and especially not STDs.